# REVENGE RIDER

# Revenge Rider

*by*

Floyd Rogers

**Dales Large Print Books**
Long Preston, North Yorkshire,
BD23 4ND, England.

British Library Cataloguing in Publication Data.

Rogers, Floyd
    Revenge rider.

    A catalogue record of this book is
    available from the British Library

    ISBN   978-1-84262-697-9 pbk

First published in Great Britain in 1964 by Robert Hale Ltd.

Copyright © 1964 Floyd Rogers

Cover illustration © Gordon Crabb by arrangement with
Alison Eldred

The moral right of the author has been asserted

Published in Large Print 2010 by arrangement with
Mr W. D. Spence

Dales Large Print is an imprint of Library Magna Books Ltd.

Printed and bound in Great Britain by
T.J. (International) Ltd., Cornwall, PL28 8RW

# ONE

Johnny Durango pulled his horse to a halt at the edge of the Cap Rock Escarpment. It had been a long ride in answer to a letter containing an urgent call from his friend whom he had not seen for eight years. He had come through the mountains of New Mexico down on to the High Plains which stretched into the Texas Panhandle. He was glad to be across the dry, arid land of whispy grass supporting herds of lean longhorns. A thousand feet below him lay pleasanter cattle country stretching away into east Texas, and less than a day's ride would see him in Newlin.

The tall, broad-shouldered cowboy eased himself in the saddle. His black shirt and black jeans which were tucked into the top of black, calf-length boots were covered with the dust of long travel. He eased his wide-brimmed, black sombrero on his head and wiped the sweat from his forehead with a handkerchief. His dark-brown eyes searched the escarpment to the right and left for a suitable way down. A few miles back he had been forced to deviate from the almost imperceptible trail, and now he reckoned it must be about two miles to his left. Johnny's long supple fingers held the reins lightly, and gently turned his horse to move along the edge of the Cap Rock.

The escarpment was rough and in parts extremely steep. Its slopes were strewn with rocks and boulders and thin sparse scrub stretched down to meet the more thickly covered plains below. Johnny had ridden about two miles when he was relieved to see a narrow path twisting its way down the terrain, which was a little less rough at this point. His horse moved carefully on to the path, and Johnny handled it gently as a nervous tremor shivered through the animal. He spoke to it softly and the horse moved steadily downwards under his gentle persuasion. Loose stones and dirt, disturbed by the animal's hoofs, showered and rolled in front of them. The path twisted and turned back and forth across the slope of the escarpment, gradually descending to the plain below, and it was over half an hour later that Johnny relaxed a little as they neared the bottom.

Suddenly the horse shied taking its rider

completely by surprise. Almost at the same moment the stillness was shattered by the crash of a rifle and a bullet whined unpleasantly close to Johnny's head. He pitched himself from the saddle crashing to the ground behind a cluster of boulders. His fingers closed round the butt of his Colt and in the same movement pulled it clear of the holster. His thoughts raced as his horse, with a frightened whinney, slid the last few feet off the path to the grassland and galloped away from the thing which had frightened it. Johnny realized that but for that he would be a dead man now; in all probability his would-be killer thought he was, so close had both things happened together. Johnny lay still. He figured his assailant might still be watching and if Johnny showed himself he would be an easy target; if he waited patiently the man might think him dead and ride away. Johnny waited, tensed for action. Who was the unknown killer? How did he know Johnny was riding this trail? Johnny searched his mind for the answers but could not find them.

Suddenly he stiffened, a movement on his left caught his attention. A cold horror chilled him to the bone when he saw a rattlesnake sliding from the path. So that was what had frightened his horse and saved his life; but now, as it moved towards the boulders, it was only a matter of seconds before it would see him and become an instrument of death. Johnny brought his gun round on to the snake watching it with a coldness in his heart, covering it until it came near enough for him to be certain of an instant kill.

His brain pounded; he knew that as soon as he squeezed the trigger his unseen attacker would know he had not been successful, but better to take a chance with an unknown assailant than to face death at the fangs of a rattler.

The snake's slithering suddenly stopped. It coiled and an ominous rattle started. It had seen him! In that instant Johnny squeezed the trigger. There was a great roar and burnt powder filled his nostrils. He watched wide-eyed the last nervous twistings as life sped from the snake. At last it was all over, the silence filled with tenseness for he knew that somewhere close by was a man geared once again into his mission of death.

Somehow he must find out where the man was. He looked round desperately, seeking some means to implement the discovery. He could not wait much longer; already the man might be circling to a more advantageous position for a second shot at Johnny. The cowboy pushed himself into a crouching position then suddenly catapulted himself forward to cross the ten yards to the next group of boulders. A rifle crashed, dust spurted at Johnny's feet, and, as he dived for the cover, a second shot splintered the rock further along the escarpment to his left. When he hit the ground he rolled over to the far end of the cover from where he quickly loosed off a shot. An answering bullet cut the dust in front of him, then almost instantaneously Johnny dived forward into a slight depression which ran across the slope. Another shot whined unpleasantly close above his head. Johnny moved quickly a few yards to his right, raised himself and fired but immediately wished he had not done so as a bullet clipped through the brim of his sombrero. Johnny dropped flat on his stomach, his chest heaving, gulping in air. The unknown man was smart and Johnny knew it was going to need all his skill to outwit the gunman. He reloaded his Colt to its capacity and removed his sombrero. After waiting a few moments Johnny raised his head carefully to peer over the edge of the hollow. He smiled to himself when he saw the muzzle of a rifle resting between two

11

boulders and pointing to a position further along the hollow. Johnny had guessed right; the killer had anticipated a move. Raising his Colt Johnny took careful aim but the distance was too great for an accurate shot. The bullet spanged the rock close to the rifle and Johnny saw it jerk round in his direction. He dropped flat in the depression and, as he started to crawl quickly to his right, a bullet whined overhead.

Johnny moved swiftly until he reached a cutting which ran up the slope at right angles to the depression. It was steep and full of stones but he reckoned if he could climb it without being seen or heard he could work his way above the unknown man. Cautiously he eased himself up and picked his way carefully, climbing up the cutting. His progress was slow as a shower of tumbling stones would give away his position. Gradually the depth of the cutting lessened and Johnny realized it was running out on to the slope which, about thirty yards further on, ended abruptly at the foot of a precipitous wall of rock rising sheer into the edge of the escarpment.

The cowboy raised himself carefully and peered over the edge of the cutting. The boulders which sheltered the killer lay some distance across the slope and slightly below Johnny's position. He was not as far above them as he would have liked and, as he examined them, he could see no sign of the man. He realized, that surrounded as the man was by huge boulders he was in a very strong position. Johnny knew he would have to get much closer, probably amongst the same boulders, before he could get the drop on his would-be assassin, but first he had to find out if the man was still there.

He picked up a piece of rock and, taking careful aim, lobbed it into the bottom of the cutting. As it crashed to the ground it sent other stones tumbling down the slope. It had the desired effect, bringing a shot whining from the boulders and giving Johnny the knowledge that the man's attention was still concentrated downwards. Almost at the same instant Johnny moved swiftly out of the cutting and dived for the cover of some rocks which stretched in a tumbled mass across the slope. He crept forward, using them as cover and thanked his luck when he saw that they widened and spilled down to the group of boulders.

Johnny reached them without mishap and straightened as he moved slowly round a boulder into a narrow cleft. He inched his way forward carefully until he found himself confronted by another narrow path running at right angles to the one on which he was standing. He peered round the huge rock. Seeing no one he started to move forward but glancing up he was startled to see his attacker lying on a flat surface above him peering between two rocks in the direction of the depression further down the slope. Johnny instinctively jumped back out of sight but in his hurry his foot scraped the surface of the rock and Johnny stumbled. Startled by the noise the unknown man twisted round, his eyes widening with surprise at the sight of Johnny Durango. Both men were off balance but Johnny's Colt came up quicker than the rifle was able to point round on to Johnny. The rocks reverberated with the roar of the Colt and the bullet caught the man full in the chest as he scrambled to his knees. His finger was already squeezing the trigger but, as he staggered under the impact of the lead, his aim was spoilt and the bullet ricocheted harmlessly off the surface of the rock close to Johnny's head. A look of disbelief seemed to cross the man's face as he fell and pitched into the cleft, to lie still a few yards from Durango.

Stepping slowly forward Johnny kept the

silent form covered with his Colt, but when he reached the man it required only a cursory glance to ascertain that he was dead. Johnny slipped his Colt back into its holster and bent down to turn the man over.

'Blackie Farrow!' he gasped recognizing the notorious hired gunman, the man who sold his ability with a gun wherever the money was right.

Johnny's thoughts raced. Why had a man of this calibre wanted to kill him? Johnny had enemies but he could think of none who would be willing to part with the price this man would demand. Who could have hired him? Had it anything to do with the letter he had received from Nick Sheridan asking him for help? If so how did Farrow and his hirer know of the contents of the letter? They must be desperate to be prepared to play a waiting watch on the trail, for Johnny had not replied to his friend so no one knew when he would be arriving.

A frown creased Johnny's brow as he pushed himself to his feet. He pulled the letter from his pocket and glanced through it, but apart from an urgent request in desperate words it told him nothing; now after this attempt on his life he realized there was much more behind Nick's appeal than he

15

had at first thought. The sooner he reached the Three Rs ranch the better.

It took Johnny a few minutes to locate Farrow's horse which he had hidden in a gully further along the hillside. Once he had the body secured across the saddle Johnny recovered his sombrero from the depression and led the ladened animal to the foot of the slope. His own horse had recovered from its fright and was gradually making its way back. Tying the reins of Blackie's animal to his own saddle horn Johnny swung on to his horse's back and, with thoughts dwelling on the possible problems ahead, he continued his journey to Newlin.

## TWO

The shadows were lengthening when Johnny Durango rode at a walking pace into the main street of Newlin. The sight of a dust-covered, travel-weary stranger leading a horse across whose saddle was slung a dead man roused the curiosity of the people on the street. They stopped and stared then began to follow slowly until, by the time Johnny pulled to a halt outside a low wooden building labelled 'Sheriff's Office', there were about thirty people gathered around him. The news of his approach had preceded him and the sheriff was already standing on the sidewalk awaiting his arrival.

Durango saw a lean man of about forty, whose hollow cheeks seemed to accentuate his thin pointed nose. His dark eyes were set deep but Johnny sensed they missed noth-ing, he could almost feel their gaze pene-trating into him. A smooth-butted Colt was strapped tightly to the sheriff's right thigh and by force of habit his long thin fingers hovered, almost unnoticed, close to the gun.

Johnny knew that because of that casualness the sheriff could out-draw most men.

When he stopped his horse Johnny leaned forward resting his hands on the saddle horn. His dark-brown eyes met the lawman's gaze unwaveringly.

'Someone didn't want me to reach town,' said Johnny quietly, 'but I guess I thought otherwise.'

The sheriff did not speak; his face was impassive as he stepped from the sidewalk. He grasped the dead man's hair, jerking his head upwards so that he could see the face. When he released his hold the head flopped downwards and the sheriff stared hard at Durango who had watched the lawman closely.

'Know him?' asked Johnny casually.

'Blackie Farrow,' drawled the sheriff.

He stepped back on to the sidewalk and nodded to two men who moved forward to take charge of the body. Johnny unfastened the reins which were tied to his saddle-horn and the two men led the horse away.

'Guess you'd better come inside,' said the sheriff and, without waiting for a reply, turned and strode into his office.

Johnny hesitated a moment before he swung slowly from the saddle, hitched his horse to the rail and, after slapping the dust from his clothes, followed the lawman into the office. The sheriff was already seated behind his desk and he indicated a chair to Johnny who flopped down, stretched his legs and eased his sombrero from the front of his head.

'Self defence, I suppose,' drawled the lawman.

'Sure,' answered Johnny. 'You'll find the bullet in his chest.'

'That doesn't necessarily mean self defence,' replied the sheriff coldly.

'With a notorious hired-gun I guess it does,' replied Johnny testily. 'It's either you or him an' he wasn't particular about his first shot.'

'Tryin' to tell me Farrow fired on you without you knowin',' said the sheriff.

'Sure,' answered Johnny. 'I was comin' down the Cap Rock when it happened.'

The lawman smiled. 'And Blackie Farrow missed you?' There was a tone of mocking incredulity in his voice.

'Even the best shots have been known to miss,' countered Johnny. 'But I suppose the real reason was that my luck was in.' Durango went on to relate his story. He studied the man carefully but was not impressed.

19

Although he searched his mind, Johnny could not recall having heard anything about the Sheriff of Newlin.

'Wal,' drawled the sheriff when Johnny had finished, 'your explanation sounds feasible but you're a stranger round these parts. Any idea why a man like Farrow should be gunning for you?'

Johnny shook his head. 'Durango's the name,' he said. 'Johnny Durango, and I don't know why Farrow should take a shot at me.' He had wondered how much to tell this lawman but, whilst he had been talking, he had decided that it would probably be better to tell him as little as possible at this stage.

'What are you doin' in Newlin?' inquired the sheriff.

'I'm afraid I'm not at liberty to tell you that,' replied Johnny.

The sheriff stiffened, his eyes narrowed looking hard at the man in front of him. 'Look here, Durango,' he snapped testily, 'I'm responsible for law and order around here; you come in with a body claiming the man took a shot at you, wal, I want to know why.'

'I wish I could answer that,' replied Johnny.

'This is a peaceful town,' went on the sheriff. 'I aim to keep it that way. If someone comes gunning for you then I figure your reasons for being here must spell trouble. My advice to you is to forget whatever you've come fer and ride on.'

Johnny looked coldly at the sheriff. 'I figure it this way,' he answered. 'You know the reputation of Blackie Farrow as a hired gun. Wal, as he tried to kill me someone around here must hev hired him.'

'Not necessarily,' retorted the sheriff.

'Smells mighty like it to me,' rapped Johnny. 'Have you seen him around town?'

'The first time I set eyes on him was when you brought him in,' came the reply.

'But you knew him,' said Johnny.

'You know as well as I do, Durango, that it's a lawman's job to know about such men,' answered the sheriff. 'And I advise you to forgit your idea that it was someone around here. I know these folks and I can't think of one who would hire a man to kill you, a stranger to these parts. It appears to me that your presence here spells trouble, so ride on, Durango, or you'll find yourself on the wrong side of the law.'

Johnny pushed himself slowly to his feet. He smiled as he looked down at the sheriff. 'Maybe you don't know your folks as well as you think.' He turned and walked to the door. With his hand on the knob he paused and looked back. 'When someone takes a shot at me, I want to know the reason why and I mean to find out!' Johnny opened the door and stepped outside leaving the sheriff glaring angrily after him.

When Johnny untied his horse from the rail there were still several people standing in groups along the street and they stared at him curiously as he rode slowly along the dust-covered road. Johnny saw a typical small, Texas town. Its unpretentious wooden buildings were in good state of repair but the section which caught his attention stood on the corner where the main north-south street cut the one along which he was riding. It advertised itself as the Gay Lady and had obviously been extended recently to take in the adjoining building. Freshly painted, it seemed to Johnny rather larger than the town required. He was tempted to slake his thirst but decided it would be better to push on and reach his destination before nightfall.

When he reached the edge of the town he put his mount into a steady trot along the west trail. A range of low hills ran in a north-east south-west direction and after riding about five miles Johnny turned on to a dirt trail which cut northwards in a steady climb. Two miles further on Johnny topped the rise and pulled his horse to a halt. The sun was low in the western sky but its rays still flooded the wide shallow valley which lay before him. It was good grassland and the dirt trail wound down the hillside to a long, neat, low ranch-house situated near the foot of the slope.

'Nick sure picked himself a nice spot,' muttered Johnny to himself admiring the position of the ranch.

His gaze swept across the surrounding countryside and he saw that the valley was bounded by only small ranges of hills of no great height and that the valley joining two great open stretches of country would have been the natural route between them had it not been for the presence of the trail he had followed to Newlin.

The sinking sun was filling the valley with the golden light of evening, and, as much as Johnny enjoyed the beauty and the silence, he wanted to reach Nick's before dark. He pushed his horse forward down the slope and before long was approaching the ranch at a steady trot. There was no sign of life as he rode past the stables, the bunkhouse and empty corrals, but as he neared the ranch-house the clop of his horse's hoofs had betrayed his arrival for he saw the door open slowly.

Johnny was taken aback when he saw a young woman, with a rifle pointing towards him, step on to the veranda. He was still a hundred yards away when she called out.

'Hold it right there, stranger or I'll blast you right out of the saddle.'

Johnny pulled his horse sharply to a halt. He knew by the tone of the voice that this woman meant what she said and he had no desire to run foul of a trigger-happy female.

'Who are you and what do you want around here?' she shouted.

'I think we could talk better if we hadn't to shout,' called Johnny.

The woman raised her gun menacingly. 'Don't move!' she yelled. Her voice was like a whiplash and Johnny froze in the saddle hardly daring to blink. 'Declare yourself,' called the woman.

Johnny was puzzled by the reception he was receiving. Where was Nick Sheridan? He saw that the only way to get to talk to this woman was to make himself known immediately.

'I'm lookin' for Nick Sheridan,' he shouted. 'Thought this was his spread. I'm Johnny Durango.'

He saw the woman stiffen momentarily, then suddenly she relaxed, the tension visibly flowing from her body. Her arms dropped slowly to her side, the rifle hanging loosely beside her as she leaned on the rail. Johnny stabbed his horse forward and whilst he covered the hundred yards at a walking pace, he studied the woman carefully.

In spite of the troubled, weary look about her he judged that she was younger than she looked at this moment, in fact he thought she would be no older than his own twenty-nine years. Her black dress was plain, its severity broken only by a small white collar about the neck. The oval face seemed to reflect recent harsh treatment by life but Johnny thought that a smile would trans-form the face and eyes which at the moment had a dull look about them. Her long hair was swept straight back and Johnny figured that if it was released from the captivity of the black ribbon at the nape of her neck it would form a pretty frame to a striking face.

He pulled to a halt beside the veranda and swung slowly from the saddle. He was aware of the woman watching him carefully as he wrapped the reins round the rail in front of the house. A faint smile which only flickered her lips greeted Johnny as he looked up.

'I'm so glad you've got here,' she said, her voice scarcely above a whisper. Her face saddened. 'But it's too late to help Nick.' The words almost choked in her throat.

Johnny looked puzzled. 'What do you mean?' he asked as he swung on the veranda. 'This is Nick Sheridan's spread, the Three Rs?'

The woman nodded. 'Yes, this is the Three Rs,' she said softly, 'but my husband is dead.'

'What!' Johnny gasped. 'Nick dead!' He stared at the woman in front of him as if he couldn't believe the news. 'You must be Kathy.'

Kathy nodded. Her eyes were full of tears as she looked at Johnny. 'I'm sorry for the reception I gave you,' she said, 'but since Nick's death I've been so afraid. But I was determined to hang on until you came; Nick had such faith in you.' Suddenly she made an effort to brighten up. 'I'm forgetting my manners, Johnny. You must be tired and hungry. Stable your horse then come inside, I'll soon have a meal ready for you.'

'Thanks,' replied Johnny. As Kathy turned to go into the house he stopped her. 'You can tell me the whole story afterwards but answer me one question now, please. Nick's death, what happened?'

Kathy looked Johnny straight in the eyes. 'A verdict of suicide, but I believe he was murdered!' she answered, and turned and hurried into the house.

Johnny stood staring after her as the door closed. A verdict of suicide; like Kathy, Johnny could not bring himself to believe that. He stepped from the veranda, untied his horse and led it to the stables where he saw that it was comfortable and had plenty of food. All the time his thoughts were going over the recent happenings. A note of urgency calling for help; his friend dead; killer obviously hired to prevent him reaching the Three Rs; a frightened widow suspicious of strangers but determined to be there when he arrived. What mystery had he ridden into? It was a thoughtful Johnny who strolled slowly back to the house from which lights shone, penetrating the immediate darkness close to the lonely ranch.

He knocked on the door, opened it and stepped inside to find himself in a square, spacious hall. There were two doors on the right hand side and one on the left whilst opposite to him another door stood ajar.

'In here, Johnny,' called Kathy.

Johnny detected a more cheerful note in

the voice even though it was only slight. He crossed the hall to the open door to find himself in a long room which ran almost the full length of the back of the house. One part was used as the kitchen and at the other end a table was set for a meal.

'You can wash there,' said Kathy indicating the sink and Johnny saw she had laid out a clean, white towel for him.

'Thanks,' he said and unbuckled his gunbelt. 'Nice place you have here,' he went on. 'I admired its position in this valley from the top of the hill as I rode in.'

Johnny started to ask questions but Kathy insisted that he ate his meal first.

Throughout the meal Johnny sensed a gradual easing in Kathy as if she was relieved to have a man about the place; someone she could trust. After the meal Kathy led the way into another room where Johnny found a blazing fire making a warm welcome.

'It is a great relief to have you here,' said Kathy. 'Nick used to talk a lot about you, and of the years spent together. How come you split up, you were still young together?'

'Wal, my folks went west,' replied Johnny, 'and I went with them. Nick and I were only twenty at the time, we'd been like brothers, never separated all our lives. Nick was coming with us, but his father died suddenly and he stayed behind with his mother. We kept in touch whenever we could by letter, but it wasn't easy when I was always on the move. As you know I'd hev been at your wedding, but when I got your letter you were already married and heading west. That was the last news I had until I received this recent letter. What was it all about Kathy? You knew Nick had written for help?'

Kathy nodded. 'Yes, I knew,' she said. 'We came west from Fort Worth as soon as we were married four years ago. Nick's mother had died and there was nothing to hold us back. Nick had always dreamed of following you westwards, but when he got married that dream changed slightly. He still wanted to go west but now to find a place to settle. We found this valley and it was just the sort of place we had dreamed about. Nick worked hard and you can see the results. Everything went right for us, longhorns thrived, no droughts, no bad winters, no trouble of any kind until…' Kathy's voice faltered and stopped. Johnny could tell the memories were troubling her.

'Take it easy, Kathy,' comforted Johnny. 'It can wait until morning if you like.'

Kathy shook her head and brushed away

the tears which were flowing in her eyes. 'It's better to get it over now, besides the sooner you know the story the better.' She paused for a moment sorting out her thoughts. 'Three months ago we received an offer for the Three Rs. It was a very good offer but we turned it down. This was the place we had made our home; we loved this valley and did not want to leave. Shortly after that things began to happen; we didn't think much about them at the time, they were small things, irritating but not of great consequence. Fences were broken, cattle strayed, horses got loose in the stable and bolted, small items were stolen and so on. A fortnight later came a second offer, better than the first, but again we decided to turn it down. Now our troubles really started. Cattle were rustled, our three cowboys shot at, beaten up. Nick suffered too; notes threatening my life were received but we decided to stick it out.'

Johnny looked thoughtful as he listened intently to Kathy. 'Who made these offers?' he asked when Kathy paused in her story.

'They were made by the lawyer in Newlin, Luke Ashton. All he would tell us was that he was acting for someone back east, someone who had been this way and taken a liking to this spread.'

Johnny nodded. 'As I expected, a bit vague,' he commented. 'Please go on, Kathy, what happened then?'

'Well, we learned that we weren't the only ones who had received offers for their ranches,' Kathy continued. 'Four others had been visited by Luke Ashton. Two of them sold out immediately. One of the others got out after his cattle took water at a poisoned hole. Dan Neale stuck out but he's had trouble same as us.'

'Didn't the sheriff do anything about it?' asked Johnny.

Kathy smiled. 'If I said no it would be a lie, but he never got any results. Nick didn't like him and reckoned his efforts were only half-hearted, as long as there was no trouble in town, he didn't seem to bother a great deal; oh, he raised posses but they never achieved anything. Nick got tired of all this and decided to take matters into his own hands and do some investigating. It was then that he wrote to you. He had great faith that with you here you could both get to the bottom of things.'

'What happened to Nick?' asked Johnny.

'He went to town one night, about ten days ago,' replied Kathy, a tightness in her voice as she recalled the events. 'He said he thought he was on to something but he would not tell me what it was; he wanted to make sure first. The next thing I heard was when the sheriff arrived to tell me Nick's body had been found in an alley next to the saloon.' Kathy's eyes were clouded as she looked at Johnny. 'They brought in a verdict of suicide.' The words choked in her throat. 'He had no reason to commit suicide, Johnny, but things got twisted at the inquest; it was said that his recent troubles must have preyed on his mind. People came forward and said Nick had drunk and gambled hard that night, that he had been with a saloon woman and had been heard to say afterwards that he could not face me again.'

'Had Nick ever done this before?' asked Johnny.

'No,' answered Kathy sharply. 'That's what was so odd about it. He liked a drink but never to go as far as they said he did. But the people who gave evidence were not of the highest character. The most damning piece of evidence was the fact that he had his own gun in his hand and one bullet had been fired.'

'How far did the sheriff probe into the matter?' requested Johnny.

'Not far,' she replied. 'The case was cut and dried; so much pointed to suicide the way things were put at the inquest.'

'I thought as much,' said Johnny, thoughtfully. 'I wasn't particularly struck by the man. What's his name?'

'Mart Webster,' said Kathy. 'But when did you meet him?'

Johnny related his encounter with Blackie Farrow and the subsequent meeting with the Sheriff of Newlin.

There was a look of concern on Kathy Sheridan's face when Johnny finished his story.

'Let's forget the whole thing, Johnny,' she said. 'I'll sell up and get out; I don't want someone else killing because of the Three Rs, and already you've...'

'Don't talk like that Kathy,' interrupted Johnny. 'You had a good enough reason to hold on until I got here, well that reason hasn't changed.'

'I know,' replied Kathy, 'but already your life's been in danger.'

'That was only to be expected when there was trouble,' continued Johnny. 'We think that Nick was murdered, and when that happens to my best friend I mean to find out why. The thing which puzzles me is how they knew I was coming here.'

'Maybe I can answer that,' answered Kathy. 'You remember I said certain things had been stolen at odd times, well there'd been a wave of petty thieving in town and the neighbouring ranches and it was always put down to that though no one was ever caught. On one occasion someone broke in here and stole several papers, nothing important, but Nick's letter to you must have been with them because when Nick looked for it to send it off to you the next day he couldn't find it and had to write another letter to you.'

Johnny looked thoughtful. 'If this petty thieving was being done by the people who wanted rid of you then they would know Nick had asked me to come and help. They would know where I was coming from by the address and therefore know my probable approach to Newlin. They were obviously prepared to play a patient, waiting game until I appeared.' He paused then looked hard at Kathy. 'Have you any idea why someone should want this land?' he asked.

Kathy shook her head. 'No,' she replied.

'There must be a good reason,' said Johnny. 'The lengths they have gone and are prepared to go to seems to indicate big stakes. If we knew what they were it may give us a lead. Kathy, if you are prepared to risk staying on here then we'll get to the bottom of this whole affair.'

'I've nowhere else to go, Johnny,' replied Kathy. 'Besides Nick loved this place so much I want to stay.'

'Then you shall!' said Johnny firmly. 'I only wish I'd got here sooner.'

# THREE

Durango had much to think about when he went to bed and, in spite of the luxurious comfort, sleep did not come easily.

The following morning he found Kathy had an appetizing breakfast ready for him, and after he had enjoyed it he talked to the three men whom Nick had hired to run the Three Rs. Johnny liked them, they were typical hard-working, tough cowboys and he admired their loyalty in staying to help Kathy, in spite of the trouble. They could shed no more light on recent events than he already knew, but he saw that in Wes Conrad, Clint Arthurs and Bud Mather he had three men ready to back him to the full in his efforts to solve the troubles which had hit the Sheridans.

During the morning Kathy rode with Johnny to Circle A spread situated eight miles west of the Three Rs, where the valley spilled out on to open country. Mrs Sheridan introduced Durango to Dan Neale and his wife, Mary, and Johnny found a couple similarly placed to the Sheridans.

'Nick and I thought alike,' pointed out Dan. 'We were not prepared to be hustled off the land we had made our home. We both love this part of Texas and were determined to stay. Of course Mary is now afraid I might get the same treatment as Nick – we are convinced it wasn't suicide – but I say if a place is worth having it's worth fighting for.'

Johnny liked this short, stocky but powerfully built man. His round red face wore a perpetual smile and Johnny saw a man who would laugh at the bad times and laugh louder when they were good, but he detected that beneath the external appearance lay a stubborn determination.

Johnny learned that the Neales had suffered similar misfortunes to the Sheridans after they had rejected the offers for the Circle A, but they could not point a finger of suspicion at anyone.

'Nick and I were determined to hold out and get to the bottom of things,' said Dan. 'He rode here before riding to Newlin on the day he died, said he hoped to have some news for me when he returned.'

'Any idea what it could have been?' asked Johnny.

'No,' came the reply, 'but I reckon he was

on to something and that's why he was killed.'

Assured of help from Dan and his two hired hands Johnny took his leave and escorted Kathy back to the Three Rs before heading for Newlin.

It was mid-afternoon when Johnny neared the sheriff's office. He observed the lawman push himself from his chair and step to the edge of the sidewalk to lean on the rail. Johnny took no notice of him and continued to ride on, looking for the building he was seeking.

'Durango!' The voice cracked the stillness like a whip. Johnny halted his horse and turned to look at the lawman through cold eyes. 'I thought I advised you to leave Newlin,' went on the sheriff.

'I only take advice when I think it is good for me,' replied Johnny a touch of cold steel in his voice.

Mart Webster stiffened. 'Don't come yelping to me if you run into trouble, which seems likely after what happened. Whoever is out to get you has probably taken precautions in case Blackie Farrow slipped up. I'm here to keep law and order but if you get in a scrape don't expect me to dig you out; I've advised you to leave town.'

Johnny looked hard at the sheriff. 'If that's your job,' he answered, 'see that you do it whatever happens!'

Webster's fingers hanging close to his Colt itched at this taunt. His eyes narrowed and his lips tightened in a hard thin line holding back his temper with an effort.

Johnny smiled and pushed his horse forward. Its slow walk hardly stirred the dust; it was the only thing which moved on the main street. Johnny could feel the tension behind him easing as he rode further away from the lawman.

Two blocks along the street he found what he was seeking and halted his horse outside an office, the door of which bore the inscription 'Luke Ashton, Lawyer.' Durango swung slowly from the saddle, wrapped the reins round the rail and, without a glance in the direction of the sheriff, knocked on the door and entered the office.

He found a man of about fifty sitting behind a desk. He was neatly dressed in a fawn frock-coat and matching trousers but Johnny noticed that these clothes had seen better times. Whilst obviously well-cared for they were worn in places. The white silk shirt and cravat tied neatly at the throat looked new. A certain distinguished look about

40

Luke Ashton was accentuated by his thin moustache and well-brushed hair, greying at the temples. As he looked up from his papers Johnny saw that Ashton's eyes were dull, as if life weighed heavily on his shoulders.

'Good afternoon, stranger,' greeted the lawyer. 'It's hot to be riding.' He mopped his forehead with a large handkerchief adding emphasis to his words. He indicated a chair to Johnny and asked as the newcomer sat down, 'What can I do for you?'

'My name's Durango, Johnny Durango,' said Johnny introducing himself. 'I'm a friend of the late Nick Sheridan and would like some information if you could give it to me.'

If Johnny expected any reaction to this announcement he was disappointed. Luke Ashton's face remained impassive.

'I was sorry about Sheridan,' replied Ashton. 'A sad case. I'll help you if I can.'

'As his friend I want to help his widow,' explained Johnny. 'I understand a very good offer was made to Nick for the Three Rs.'

'That's right,' confirmed Ashton. 'I strongly advised Sheridan to accept, but he wouldn't.'

'You advised him to take the offer?' said Johnny a note of curiosity in his voice. 'But if you were making the offer on behalf of someone I wouldn't have thought it was your job to advise the seller as well.'

'Well, er … I … er…' spluttered the lawyer somewhat caught off his guard. 'I meant it was such a good offer that I thought it was in Sheridan's interest to accept.'

Johnny nodded as if accepting Ashton's explanation. 'Might I ask who was making these bids to buy the Three Rs?'

Ashton smiled wryly. 'I'm afraid I'm not at liberty to disclose the name of the person,' he replied. 'He's from the east and wanted a place out here as an escape from business worries.'

'Does the offer still stand?' asked Johnny.

'Certainly,' answered the lawyer. 'The papers can soon be drawn up should Mrs Sheridan decide to sell, but I'm afraid my client may look elsewhere if she doesn't decide soon. In fact he's already told me to look around but I told him to wait a short while; let Mrs Sheridan get over the shock of this tragic affair and she may decide to sell.'

'I believe other tracts of land have been purchased recently,' said Durango. 'Did you put those deals through?'

'Yes,' nodded the lawyer. 'But if you're thinking they were all connected, you're mistaken.'

'Just one other question. I'd like you to answer,' said Johnny. 'Did Nick Sheridan visit you that last day he was in town?'

'No,' returned Ashton. He paused a moment. 'Curiosity seems to be part of your make up,' he added with a smile.

'Not curiosity alone,' replied Johnny coldly. 'A love of the truth and justice makes me naturally curious when I think they are missing.' He pushed himself to his feet. 'Good day to you, Mister Ashton, and thank you.' He turned sharply and walked from the office leaving a man, whose thoughts were mixed, pulling nervously at his moustache.

Johnny turned along the sidewalk then walked across the street towards the bank, aware that the sheriff, seated outside his office, was watching him. When he entered the bank he introduced himself to the clerk and asked to see the bank manager. A few moments later he was ushered into the manager's office where he was greeted by a smiling, red-faced man of about fifty. He took Johnny's hand in a firm grip.

'What can I do for you, Mister Durango?' he asked indicating a chair.

Johnny liked the look of this man and when he sat down he came straight to the point.

'I'm a friend of Nick and Kathy Sheridan,' he said. 'I'm not satisfied with the verdict on Nick's death so I'm doing some investigating apart from seeing that Kathy's interests are protected at this time. I'm wondering if you can throw any light on the matter.'

'I doubt it,' replied the bank manager. 'Although I must say I was surprised at what happened that night. Nick had been to see me earlier that day and he...'

'He came into Newlin to see you!' gasped Johnny excitedly. 'He told no one why he was coming into town, but now if you know it may throw a completely new light on the affair.'

'Hold hard, Durango,' hastened the official. 'His visit to me may not have been his only reason for coming to town and as far as I can see it had no bearing on what happened later. I was surprised at what happened because Nick was in high spirits when he saw me and I would have said that suicide was far from his mind.'

'Why did he come to see you?' asked Johnny.

The bank manager looked at his hands thoughtfully. 'My clients' affairs are strictly private but I think in this case I might waive that rule for once,' he said. 'I like the look of you, Durango, and I feel there is something happening around Newlin which is not altogether straight.' Seeing questions springing to Johnny's lips he hastened to add. 'I can't tell you what; it's just a feeling I've had for a little while. Everything seems fair and square but suddenly for no apparent reason there's been a lot of dealing in land. Don't get me wrong, there's been nothing crooked about it. It has all been done through Luke Ashton, Newlin's lawyer; terms have been agreed and cash has been paid to those folks who have been selling. Everything has been above board as far as I can see.'

'Had Nick's visit to you something to do with this?' pressed Johnny.

'I'm coming to that,' replied the bank manager. 'Nick wanted to know if he could have a loan to buy more land. Well his account was good and I agreed.'

'Where was this land he wanted to buy?' asked Durango.

'He said he would tell me later,' answered the official. 'But when I agreed to the loan he seemed highly delighted and said, that now he would be able to blow things sky-high.'

Johnny looked puzzled. 'Do you think that there was any connection between that remark and what happened afterwards?' he asked.

'Well, he certainly blew things sky-high,' said the bank official, 'but somehow when I think back I don't believe he was referring to what he did later that night. I think Nick had found something out about these land deals; look at it this way; all these deals had been negotiated through Ashton for someone outside of Newlin then along comes Sheridan wanting to buy land and apparently proposing to do the deal on his own.'

'I see your implication,' agreed Johnny. 'It's a great pity Nick didn't discuss it more fully with you. Maybe somebody didn't like him knuckling in. He was made an offer for the Three Rs you know.'

It was the turn of the bank official to be surprised. 'I didn't know about that,' he said. 'Seems as though someone is interested in a lot of land around here.'

Johnny pushed himself to his feet. 'Thank you very much for your help,' he said. 'I am staying with Mrs Sheridan and if you think of anything else which might help me I'd be mighty grateful if you would let me know.'

'I certainly will,' said the bank manager and extended a friendly hand to Johnny who took it in a firm grip.

Luke Ashton bit his lip nervously as he watched Johnny Durango from the window of his office cross the road to enter the bank. Immediately the young cowboy had disappeared into the building, Ashton grabbed his hat and hurried from his office slamming the door behind him in his haste. He walked swiftly along the sidewalk, almost breaking into a run as he headed for the saloon.

When the sheriff saw the lawyer leave his office in such a rush he shoved himself from his chair and strolled across the sun-drenched street timing his arrival at the saloon to coincide with that of Luke Ashton's.

'Howdy, Luke,' greeted Mart Webster casually. 'You're in a rush.'

Ashton glanced sharply at the lawman. 'You'd better come with me and hear what I have to tell Curt,' he answered, a note of invitation in his voice, as if he envied the casual manner of Webster.

He pushed open the saloon door and crossed to the bar followed by the sheriff.

'Give me a whisky,' he called to the barman. 'Do you want one?' he asked the sheriff who stood beside him leaning on the bar. The lawman shook his head. 'Is Curt Simpson in?' queried Ashton when the barman brought his drink.

'He's up in his room,' replied the barman.

Ashton plucked at the glass, drained it in one gulp and without a word hurried to the staircase which led to the balcony. The sheriff followed him and a few moments later both men entered Curt Simpson's room.

The big, bulky man was seated behind a huge oak desk and, when he saw who his visitors were, leaned back in his chair and greeted them amiably. The chair creaked under his fifteen stone as he leaned forward, picked up a box from the desk, opened the lid and held it out to each man in turn.

'Something bothering you, Ashton?' asked Simpson when he observed the lawyer's hand shaking as he took a cheroot from the box. Simpson's voice matched his huge frame and seemed to boom from the massive, barrel-shaped chest and broad, thick-set neck.

'Everything was fair and square until this murder,' spluttered the lawyer, 'and I want you to remember I was all against that; I wanted no part of that sort of thing. Now someone's asking questions.'

The sheriff had casually struck a match and held it for Curt Simpson to light his cheroot. He did this with meticulous care as he watched Ashton closely. The lawyer drew nervously on his cheroot waiting for Simpson to answer. The sheriff was about to light his cheroot when he blew out the match and struck another; the third light off the same match was unlucky.

Curt grinned. 'You and your superstitions, Mart, watch they aren't your undoing. Who's asking questions?' The query was shot at the lawyer so suddenly that he jumped nervously.

'Johnny Durango,' spluttered Ashton.

Simpson glanced sharply at Webster. 'Seems he didn't take your warning seriously yesterday,' he observed.

'Looks like it,' drawled the sheriff. 'I've warned him again this morning.'

'What are we going to do about him?' asked the lawyer. 'We can't have him nosing around.'

'I hope you didn't act like this in front of him,' snorted Simpson contemptuously.

'No, no, Curt, I didn't,' replied Ashton. 'It's only when I start thinking about it that I get like this.'

'Then don't think!' rapped Curt. 'You just do as you're told.'

'When he left, Durango went to the bank,'

pointed out Mart. 'If Mike Hardy tells him that Sheridan was trying to borrow money to buy land it might give Durango a lead.'

'Very little to go on,' replied Simpson. 'Remember we made sure no one else knew about Sheridan's plans before he was killed; Ruth was certain he hadn't told anyone so it's hardly likely that Durango will get on to it through anything the bank manager can tell him. If only that fool Farrow hadn't slipped up; it means that some of our own boys are going to have to deal with Durango.'

'That's bringing it too near home,' replied the sheriff. 'A hired killer way out at the Cap Rock was one thing. I could close my eyes to that but as Sheriff of Newlin I'd have to dig deeper if something happened here. I stalled over Sheridan's death but it's not going to be easy to do that again. Rough him up a bit outside of town and he might start to think seriously about my warning.'

Simpson looked thoughtful. 'Maybe you're right, Mart. We don't want to attract too much attention now with another killing. It looks as if Durango is trying to follow Sheridan's movements that day so no doubt he'll be paying a call here. I'll get three of the boys to deal with him when leaves. Ashton you get out to the Three Rs, make Kathy Sheridan another offer; I guess Durango must have stayed there last night and if he turns up worse for wear and she's had another offer then it might just persuade them to sell.'

Ashton nodded and he and Webster left Simpson. They paused outside the door and surveyed the large room from the balcony. Seeing no sign of Durango they hurried from the saloon. Luke Ashton made his way quickly to the livery stable for his horse and left Newlin by the west road. Mart Webster was back in his chair outside his office by the time Durango came out of the bank.

Durango paused on the sidewalk outside the bank. He was disappointed that he had not got a more positive lead on Nick Sheridan's problems, but he felt he had made at least some headway with the information presented to him by the bank manager. It seemed obvious to Johnny that these land deals were being made with some ulterior motive and whoever was making them was prepared to deal drastically with anyone who got in the way. But he realized he was no nearer solving the problem as to why the land was being bought and who was buying it.

Johnny started to saunter across the road towards the saloon. His mind was on Nick's last visit to town, maybe he could find some answer to Nick's actions in the Gay Lady.

Suddenly there was a thunder of hoofs and a horse tore out of a side street next to the saloon. Startled, Johnny glanced over his shoulder. The animal, its rider having difficulty in controlling it, was almost on top of him. Johnny flung himself sideways in a desperate bid to avoid the rushing animal. He felt a heavy blow in the middle of his back as the horse's side added to his momentum and sent him flying across the street to crash into the edge of the sidewalk. A searing pain shot through his arm and down his side; the breath was driven from his body as he flopped on to the hard ground and lay still, gasping for breath. The pound of hoofs gradually faded as the animal tore along the street out of town.

Sheriff Mart Webster jumped to his feet and raced to Johnny who was struggling to sit up when the lawman reached him. Mart helped the dazed and shaken man to his feet.

'That was a close shave, Durango,' observed Webster.

Johnny looked wryly at the sheriff. 'See who it was?' he muttered.

'No,' answered Mart. 'I was dozing in the

chair and it all happened so quickly. That horse sure was giving some trouble.'

Johnny leaned against the rail on the sidewalk holding his throbbing side. 'I reckon that horse wasn't really out of control an' that was no accident.'

'Deliberate?' The sheriff sounded surprised although he reckoned that Curt Simpson must have decided on this action after he and Ashton had left the Gay Lady.

'Sure,' replied Johnny wincing as he straightened himself. His back felt as if it had been hit with a sledgehammer. 'Someone thinks it would be better if I wasn't around here.'

'Wal, if you want to look at it that way, remember I advised you to keep goin' when you arrived yesterday,' pointed out Webster.

Johnny looked at the lawman wondering if he knew more about this attempt to run him down than he cared to admit and yet how could he, he'd been sat outside his office all the time unless – Johnny's thoughts were interrupted by Webster.

'I reckon you ought to let the Doc check you over,' he said. 'I'll take you; think you can walk that far?'

Johnny nodded. 'Thanks,' he said.

Ten minutes later, stripped to the waist, he

was laid out on a couch in Doc Fleming's. After a thorough examination the doctor announced that except for some bad bruises Johnny was all right.

'Good,' remarked the sheriff. 'I'll see if I can find any information for your suspicions, Durango. Don't forget my advice to you.'

As the door closed behind him Johnny wondered if the sheriff's efforts would be as good as those he appeared to have made after Nick Sheridan's death.

# FOUR

When Johnny left Doc Fleming's he headed for the saloon. His body ached and his better judgement told him to return to the Three Rs but Johnny could not get it out of his mind that the rider had come out of the side street next to the Gay Lady and that it was at the Gay Lady that Nick's trouble appeared to have started on his last day in town.

He pushed open the door of the saloon to find himself in a big room one end of which was occupied by a stage. The opposite end was taken up by gambling tables and the space in between was filled with small tables. Johnny strolled slowly to the long, shiny mahogany counter, behind which the wall was fitted with a mirror of the same length. Durango called for a beer and, leaning with his back to the bar, looked round the room. It was gaudily painted in several colours and on the wall opposite to him were several paintings of voluptuous, semi-naked females. The imposing curved staircase, bordered by a finely carved banister, led to a balcony which gave access to several rooms. Johnny turned back to the bar when his drink arrived.

'Mighty imposing place you've got here,' he observed.

'Sure is,' grinned the barman. 'Biggest and best in the west of Texas.'

'Let's hope you get more custom than this to keep it open,' Johnny muttered to himself when the barman moved away.

The few people in the room were lost in its vastness and Johnny figured that even if all the saloon visitors in Newlin and the surrounding district came in there would still be plenty of room. The Gay Lady looked out of proportion to the rest of this quiet Texas town. It puzzled Johnny why such a place should have been built; it was as if someone expected a boom, but where was the boom coming from in cattle country?

Johnny enjoyed his drink and, when he had finished it, he called the barman over.

'I'd like to meet the man who runs such a place as this,' he said. 'I reckon I could put some business his way.'

'I'll see if Mr Simpson will see you,' replied the barman. 'He's always interested in a business deal.'

The barman hurried away and Johnny watched him climb the stairs and noted the room which he entered from the balcony. If an invitation to an interview was not forthcoming Johnny was determined to force it, but drastic action was not necessary, for, when the barman returned he pointed out Curt Simpson's room and told Johnny to go up.

Johnny was surprised at the elegant furnishings when he entered the room but was even more surprised at the huge bulk of the man who came forward to greet him. Curt Simpson was smartly dressed in a grey frock-coat and matching trousers and Johnny noted the gun-belt strapped around his waist, the Colt hidden by the length of the coat. Durango felt the power of his grip as they shook hands and exchanged names. Simpson smiled a greeting but Johnny felt no warmth in the smile. In fact he saw a coldness in the eyes and knew this man could be merciless in his quest for what he wanted, and yet he felt that he probably lacked the necessary subtleties to play for big deals. The shrewd, calculating brain required for the master was probably lacking and Johnny was determined to find out if his supposition was correct.

'Now I hear you have a proposition, Durango,' said Simpson indicating a chair to Johnny as he moved to his own seat behind the desk.

Johnny smiled. 'I owe you an apology,' he explained. 'I didn't think you would see me unless I put it that way. I have no deal to put to you but you may be able to help me.'

Curt Simpson stiffened. This was what he had expected but he had to make a pretence of being annoyed. 'That was most ungentlemanly of you,' he said coldly. 'You realize I'd be justified in having you thrown out.'

'I guess you would,' agreed Johnny, 'but I hope you won't; I hope you'll be kind enough to answer some questions.' Johnny played it smoothly making it sound as if Simpson would be doing him a great favour. He figured this way would give the saloon owner a sense of power which Johnny reckoned he liked.

'Well,' answered Simpson condescendingly, 'I guess that now you're here you may as well say your piece.'

'I'm a friend of Nick Sheridan's,' said Johnny watching Simpson closely, hoping he might see some reaction from the saloon owner but the hard face remained expressionless. 'I was surprised to find he was dead when I arrived here yesterday but what surprised me even more was that he committed suicide. Nick wasn't a man like that and I was hoping a few answers to some questions might ease my mind about his death – was it accidental? Maybe a gun in his hand accidentally went off, you know, something like that.' Johnny did not want to give this man the impression that he wanted to dig too deeply, otherwise he reckoned Simpson would not say very much.

Curt had studied Durango as he was speaking and he was surprised to find that the cowboy had taken such an easy line, but if his thoughts were drifting that way then maybe they needed encouraging.

'I guess that could have happened,' agreed Simpson. 'I suppose the verdict of suicide was based largely on what he said in the saloon that night. Sheridan's actions were right out of keeping with the man. He liked a drink but went to extremes that night and of course as you know drink can have strange effects on a man who is not used to it.'

'What happened?' asked Johnny.

'Sheridan was full of beans when he came in,' explained Simpson. 'He said he had a big land deal coming off and had just settled a loan from the bank. He seemed to want to celebrate and had a few drinks. They took effect very quickly. Sheridan spotted the gambling tables and figured he could manage without that loan from the bank. He had a considerable amount of money on him. For a time he was lucky but then things went wrong. He lost all he had; got me to loan him more in IOUs and finally lost that. He tried to find solace in more drink, and shortly after that I saw him being helped upstairs by one of the saloon girls. When he reappeared about a couple of hours later he had sobered up a little; he was very morose; I suppose the full impact of what he had done had made itself felt and it hurt even more because his actions had been so out of character. I don't think I have ever seen a man so miserable with himself. He said he could not face his wife again; he left the saloon; two hours later he was found in the alley dead with his own gun in his hand, one bullet fired.'

Johnny had listened intently but apart from being a more detailed description it fitted with what he already knew. There was nothing to indicate that Curt Simpson had any connection with Nick's death, but still Johnny was puzzled.

'Have you still got those IOUs?' asked Johnny.

'Yes,' replied Simpson. 'I felt that I couldn't present them to Kathy Sheridan so soon after Nick's death.'

'That was mighty thoughtful of you,' said Johnny.

'Help people and you always get help, I say,' replied Simpson with a smile.

Johnny rose to his feet. 'I guess I'll push along,' he said. 'Thanks for your help but it looks to me as if the suicide verdict was correct; Nick certainly seems to have gone off the rails for once.' He shook hands with Simpson who crossed the room to the door with Johnny. 'It's a mighty fine place you've got here,' remarked Johnny, 'but a bit on the big side for such a place as Newlin.'

'Maybe,' replied Curt. 'But I'm a big man, I like my places big. Just made some extensions and had the place done up.'

'Well, I hope it pays off,' said Johnny casually.

'I reckon it will,' answered Simpson. He opened the door and after saying good-bye to Johnny he watched the cowboy leave the saloon. As soon as Johnny had disappeared Simpson hurried down the stairs and crossed the room quickly to three cowboys and a saloon girl who were sitting at a table in one corner.

'Beat it, Margie,' snapped Simpson as he strode up. His tone was harsh and the girl reluctantly strolled from the table. She knew better than to disobey the big man but there was a flash of hate in her eyes as she moved away. Simpson glared angrily at one of the men. 'You muffed it, Red,' he snarled.

'He moved fast,' put in Red, quickly making his excuse. 'Even so the horse caught him. I was surprised to see him come...'

'There's no time for excuses,' interrupted Curt harshly. 'The three of you get after him but you can't make the job permanent. Run down by an uncontrollable horse could be classified as an accident but this couldn't. Give him a good going over and make it clear that worse could happen if he stays around here.'

The three men nodded, drained their glasses and hurried from the saloon in time to see Johnny Durango unhitching his horse from the rail outside the lawyer's office, where he had left it when he first arrived in town. They leaned casually on the rail and watched Johnny leave Newlin by the west road. Once the cowboy was clear of town they climbed on their horses and followed.

Keeping at a respectable distance they stuck cautiously to his trail. When Durango turned off the west road on to the dirt trail heading towards the hills the three men swung into a shallow gully and pushed their horses into a gallop in order to out-ride Johnny. They kept the animals to a fast pace and when they reached the hill they used the cover of boulders to make their way unseen to the edge of the trail.

Red swung from the saddle and scrambled amongst a group of huge boulders until he had a view of the countryside below. When he spotted Johnny he rejoined his companions.

'He's comin' at a steady pace,' Red announced. 'Be here in about five minutes.'

The men secured their horses out of sight and, pulling their neckerchiefs over the lower half of their faces, edged their way close to the trail. With Colts drawn they waited for a clop of a horse's hoofs to herald the approach of Johnny Durango.

Johnny was lost in his thoughts as he rode steadily back to the Three Rs. He had not gained as much information as he had hoped from his visit to Newlin but from what the bank manager had said Nick must have found something out about the land deals. Simpson had not told him much and yet two of his remarks, innocent on the surface, could easily have deeper meanings if looked at closely. They kept thrusting themselves into his mind; the drinks had taken effect on Nick quickly and Simpson reckoned the elaborate Gay Lady would pay off. There seemed no connection between the remarks but for some reason they had stuck in Johnny's mind.

He started the climb up the hillside when suddenly he was shaken out of his thoughts by the appearance of three masked men in his path. His hand flew towards his Colt but froze before he had touched it. He was covered by three guns and knew it was no good to draw against those odds. Tempted to spur his horse into a gallop he resisted, realizing he could be shot down before he had covered a few yards.

One man stepped forward and seized the horse's reins. 'Git down,' he snapped.

Johnny swung slowly from the saddle. A second man moved forward and then relieved Durango of his gun whilst the first turned the horse and, with a sharp slap on its hind quarters, sent it galloping back down the slope. Johnny's thoughts raced; another attack upon him; someone was keen to have him out of the way and yet why hadn't they gunned him down?

Two men shoved their Colts back into their holsters whilst the third kept him covered. They moved menacingly towards him. Suddenly one of them stepped swiftly sideways and as Johnny automatically half turned the first leaped forward smashing his broad, hairy fist into the side of Johnny's face. Johnny staggered backwards and both men jumped after him. One moved behind him and before Durango could recover the man had pinioned his arms in a vice-like grip. The other man smashed his fist into Johnny's side where he had already suffered pain from his encounter with the horse in Newlin. Pain stabbed through his body and Johnny cried out in agony. A fist crashed into his stomach driving the breath out of him. He tried to double-up but the grip held him firm, and, as it tightened, Johnny's arm, bruised by the Newlin sidewalk, throbbed with pain. Johnny's brain reeled as an open hand slapped him hard across the face drawing blood from the corner of his mouth.

'You are not wanted around here,' hissed a voice in his ear. 'When we've finished with you remember you can get worse, so ride an' don't come back.'

'You are not wanted.' As if to add emphasis to the words the man in front of him

65

repeated his actions and searing pain lanced through his body. Suddenly the man behind him released his grip and punched him in the back. His body had ached there ever since the horse had knocked him and now he felt as if the animal was upon him again. Johnny staggered forward to meet a powerful fist full on the face. His head jerked backwards; his brain spun and he reeled sideways to fall against a boulder. The ground spun before his eyes and a pounding blow in his side propelled him forward, face downwards on the ground. He was almost oblivious to the blow on the back of the neck which dispatched him into complete darkness.

It was about two hours later that some sort of sense began to penetrate Johnny Durango's brain. First he was aware that his face was pressing against the ground and then he felt one big ache throughout his body, as if a herd of longhorns had tramped over him. He did not move; reason came slowly to his mind. His face felt puffed and sore and it seemed a tremendous effort to open one eye. He realized it was still light. As feeling came back into his brain and body slowly, he wished it hadn't, for as his brain cleared he began to feel the effects of his beating.

Johnny tried to push himself up but the effort was too much and he flopped back to the ground, gasping with the struggle. Five minutes passed before he tried again and this time he succeeded in rolling over on to his back. He lay spreadeagled, breathing deeply. Slowly he opened his eyes and immediately shut them again to keep out the glare from the burning blue sky.

How long he lay there Johnny never knew but next time he opened his eyes the glare was not so harsh. His head throbbed; his face burned, and his whole being ached. Johnny raised an arm slowly and touched his face. His forehead felt as if a fire burned in it; blood had dried and caked from two nasty cuts on his cheek and mouth. With a great effort Johnny pushed himself to his feet. His head swam and, as he straightened, he staggered. He found support against a boulder and, inching forward, sought comfort in its shadow. In spite of the throbbing his head cleared and a few minutes later he looked around for his horse. It was standing at the bottom of the slope champing grass. Mustering his energy, Johnny walked towards the animal, pausing only to retrieve his sombrero and gun. Once he was moving he was reluctant to stop for each step was a movement of pain and he knew it would be difficult to start again.

When he reached his horse he paused, resting against its side, trying to retrieve some of his spent energy. A few minutes later he grasped the saddle-horn and hauled himself on to the horse's back. He almost passed out from the pain which ripped through his side after the exertion. When his mind cleared he tapped the animal with his heels and sent it forward up the slope at a walking pace.

The movement of the horse was not easy on his bruised body and he was thankful when he reached the Three Rs ranch-house. Halting against the veranda he half slipped and half fell from the saddle hitting the woodwork with a thud. Johnny was struggling to his feet when the front door was flung open and Kathy appeared. She gasped with surprise and horror at seeing Johnny in such a condition but hastened to help him into the house.

'What happened?' she asked, deep concern in her voice.

'Later,' panted Johnny.

Kathy helped him to his bedroom where he flopped exhausted on to the bed.

'I'll be back in a minute,' called Kathy, as

she hurried from the room. She ran to the bunkhouse and returned a few moments later with Wes Conrad and Clint Arthurs, whilst Bud Mather raced to the stables for a horse to head for town for Doc Fleming.

Wes and Clint soon had Johnny undressed and into bed. Kathy heated some water and bathed his wounds carefully. By the time Doc Fleming arrived Johnny was feeling much more comfortable. The doctor gave him a thorough examination for the second time that day and announced that there was nothing seriously wrong with him.

'You've a strong constitution, young man,' he said. 'A couple of days complete rest should set you on your feet again but your side will be painful for a few days, there's severe bruising there.'

Johnny slept well that night, and the next morning when Kathy brought him his breakfast, he felt much better. Johnny told his story and when he had finished there was a look of concern on Kathy's face.

'We can't go on like this, Johnny,' she said. 'Two attempts on your life and a severe beating; it's too much to ask you to go on risking your life for the sake of the Three Rs.' Johnny started to protest but Kathy stopped him. 'Whilst you were in town

69

yesterday Luke Ashton came out here and made me another offer. I turned it down but now after what has happened to you I'm going to ride into town and accept.'

'Kathy, you can't!' answered Johnny. 'You must hang on – remember what you told me about this being your home; this was the place you and Nick wanted.'

'What's happened is finished,' replied Kathy. 'Nick can't come back and I'm not going to have you killed because I want to stop here.'

'Don't talk like that, Kathy,' insisted Johnny; 'Nick was my best friend; I want to help his wife, and clear up all the claims that he committed suicide. Even if you sell out I will stay to do just that so you may as well hang on to the Three Rs.'

# FIVE

Although Johnny tried hard to persuade Kathy to let him get up, she insisted that he follow the doctor's advice.

When Kathy brought him some coffee during the morning he asked her if Nick had ever talked about buying more land. Kathy was surprised by the question and was even more surprised when Johnny told her that Nick had paid a visit to the bank manager with a view to borrowing money for that purpose.

'He never told me about it,' said Kathy, 'and I'm sure he would have done if that had been his intention; we always discussed all our plans together. Besides we decided some time ago that the ranch was as big as we wanted.'

Johnny looked thoughtful. 'Maybe it was only a blind. With all this land buying going on he let it be known that he was proposing to buy some in order to force someone's hand.'

'If that is so, he succeeded only too well,'

71

murmured Kathy. 'There is one thing,' she added as if she had suddenly remembered it, 'Nick had spent some time lately studying maps of this area.'

'Have you still got them?' asked Johnny excitedly. 'Maybe they will help us.'

Kathy hurried away to return a few minutes later with two maps. One was a general map of the area showing the topography of the district with the trails clearly marked whilst the other had various sections marked off.

'Those are the ranches in the area,' said Kathy and went on to tell him about them.

Johnny saw that the Three Rs occupied all the valley whilst Dan Neale's Circle A bordered it at the west end. The east side ran into two small spreads which had been sold recently. To the north side of the west road from Newlin lay a very large ranch run by a tough middle-aged man who had been one of the first to move into the district and was already ranching on a large scale when the Sheridans set up the Three Rs.

'Had any trouble from him?' asked Johnny.

Kathy shook her head. 'No,' she replied. 'In fact he helped us when we arrived here. He always said he had all the land he wanted.'

'Who owns this spread?' questioned Johnny

pointing to a large area marked on the map to the north of the Three Rs. It embraced the hills to the north and spread westwards to the leveller country.

'That's the Twisted F,' said Kathy. 'It's owned by someone called Amos North. We've never met him; I don't think he spends much time there as he is supposed to have more land in New Mexico and more to the east in Baylor County. He has a good crew who run the Twisted F efficiently.'

Throughout the morning Johnny studied the maps but there was nothing to indicate which section of land had attracted Nick. Johnny began to think more and more that Nick's proposed buy had been voiced to make someone show his hand. Throughout that day and the succeeding one he had much to think about, going over and over in his mind all he knew and trying to link people and facts. Some of the answers he felt lay at the Gay Lady and it was to there that he returned on his first day out of bed.

When the barman came to greet him Johnny asked if he could point out the saloon girl known as Ruth.

'Sure,' came the reply and the man called along the bar to a girl at the far end.

The girl walked slowly towards the cowboy who had asked for her, eyeing him up and down. 'Howdy, stranger,' she greeted. 'What do you want with me?' There was a teasing smile in her deep brown eyes.

'Care to join me in a drink?' he said.

Ruth smiled her approval and Johnny called for a bottle and two glasses.

'Let's use a table,' he said and, as the girl led the way across the room, he admired her shapely figure which was shown to advantage by the shoulderless, calf-length dress drawn tight at the waist. Her dark hair was piled high on her head and, as they sat down, Johnny noted a certain hardness about her face. Johnny poured two drinks then looked straight at the girl.

'I believe you spent some time with Nick Sheridan on the night of his murder,' said Johnny coming straight to the point. 'I'd like to know about it.'

The girl stiffened; her eyes went cold. This was not what she had expected from this cowboy. She shrugged her shoulders.

'There's nothing to tell,' she said. 'What does a man want with a girl like me?'

'I figure that question should be what did you want with a man like Nick Sheridan?' rapped back Johnny. 'What Nick did that night was completely out of character so didn't you…'

'Look, mister,' cut in the girl harshly, 'if his own woman can't hold him it's not unknown for a man to find comfort in me.'

'It wasn't like that with Nick and Kathy Sheridan,' answered Johnny. His thoughts had been racing; he had detected that Ruth had been shaken by his inferences but she had covered up quickly. He had decided that the only way to get anywhere in this whole business was to force the play and he decided that now was the time to make the first move. 'Nick Sheridan came in here in high spirits and I figure you had to find out how much he knew.'

The girl drew herself up haughtily; her eyes narrowed, anger smouldering in them. 'I don't know what you are talking about,' she snapped. 'Nick Sheridan came in here for a good time and he got it.'

'Too good,' answered Johnny. 'So good that he was found dead a short time afterwards.'

'Suicide,' hissed Ruth. 'I can't help it if a man is filled with remorse after an evening out and is frightened to face his wife.'

'Nick wasn't afraid of Kathy,' snapped Johnny. The girl started to push herself from the table but Durango reached forward and grabbed her wrist tightly. 'Sit down,' he hissed, 'I haven't finished yet. I figure Nick had that night forced upon him, someone was frightened of him and when you found out how much he knew he was murdered.'

Ruth gasped staring wide-eyed at Johnny. 'Murdered?' she cried, feigning surprise. 'You don't know what you are talking about. What are you tying to drag me into?' Johnny detected a covering up of alarm in the girl and he reckoned he had not been far off the mark in his supposition. 'I'll get you thrown out of here!' Her voice had risen shrilly. She jumped to her feet dragging her wrist free from Johnny's grasp. Her chair flew over backwards hitting the floor with a crash. She looked round anxiously.

It was then that Johnny noticed Curt Simpson for the first time. He was standing on the balcony looking down into the saloon. He had not been there when Durango had entered the Gay Lady and Johnny had been so intent on talking to Ruth that he had not noticed the saloon owner appear on the balcony.

Johnny and Ruth had just sat down at the table when Curt Simpson emerged from his room and surveyed the customers in the room below. His lips tightened, and his eyes smouldered angrily when he saw Johnny Durango talking to Ruth. He cursed under his breath and, swinging round, barged back into his room where Red and one of his sidekicks were sitting.

'Durango's out there,' he stormed. 'The beating up he got from you hasn't persuaded him to leave. Get down there and find some pretext to take him, this time for keeps.'

The two men slid out of the room and, seeing Johnny taken up with Ruth, moved down the stairs without being noticed.

'I'll watch for an openin', take your cue from me,' whispered Red and indicated to his companion to move slowly. Red leaned on the rail at the bottom of the staircase and, glancing upwards, noticed that Curt Simpson had appeared on the balcony. He turned his attention to Durango and stiffened when he saw the cowboy grab Ruth's wrist.

Suddenly Ruth jumped up sending her chair crashing to the floor. She looked round anxiously. This was just the chance he needed. Red strode forward quickly.

'This hombre annoyin' you, Ruth,' he asked eyeing Johnny with a hostile look.

'Sure is Red, he wants throwing out,' cried Ruth.

Johnny had risen to his feet. This type of

man does not act on his own he thought, but as he glanced round he realized that Red's accomplice could be any of the men in the room.

'Alright stranger, on your way, we don't like your type around here,' snarled Red.

Johnny hesitated and in that instant Red's hand flashed to his Colt. The gun cleared the leather but his finger was only squeezing the trigger when he staggered under the impact of the lead from Johnny's Colt with the result that his aim was off the mark. The bullet ripped through Johnny's shirt nicking his arm. Almost at the same instant as he fired Johnny flung himself sideways knowing that from somewhere in the room another gun would bark.

As he hit the floor wood splintered, torn from the table above his head by the bullet meant for him. Johnny rolled over and a second bullet hit the floor where he had been only a moment before. Johnny had rolled clear of the table and it brought the gunman into sight. Even as he brought his gun round to bear on Johnny, Durango fired. The man staggered backwards crashing against a table. He clutched at his stomach, his face contorted in agony. Johnny fired again and the man spun round to crash to the floor and lay still.

Everything had happened so quickly and now all that was left was the blue gunsmoke drifting lazily on the silent air. Suddenly the unnatural quietness was shattered as the door burst open and Sheriff Mart Webster raced in with gun drawn. His gaze took in the scene at a glance and he moved quickly towards Johnny.

As Durango climbed to his feet he found himself gazing into the muzzle of a Colt in the hand of the lawman.

'Durango, you're under arrest!' snapped the sheriff grabbing Johnny's Colt.

'It was self-defence, sheriff,' protested Johnny. 'There are plenty of witnesses.'

The sheriff glanced round the people in the saloon and seeing the number of nods he received he handed Johnny's Colt back to him.

His eyes narrowed as he looked hard at Johnny. 'Durango,' he said. 'I warned you I wanted no trouble in this town; if you choose to hang around here and there's more trouble I might just arrest you for disturbing the peace.'

'Then you might just have to do that, sheriff,' returned Johnny. 'I aren't leavin'; as a matter of fact I might be askin' you to re-open the case of Nick Sheridan's death.'

His voice was loud enough for all to hear and the fact that the sheriff shot a quick nervous glance at Curt Simpson was not lost upon Johnny.

The lawman quickly composed himself. 'That case is closed,' rapped Webster. 'Don't try to play the law in this town. Best thing you can do is to git that arm seen to and put Newlin behind you.'

Johnny said nothing, picked up his sombrero and strode from the saloon. He hurried along the sidewalk to Doc Fleming's.

'You are always wanting me,' said the doctor as he examined the wound. 'Trouble seems to follow you around.'

'There might be more before I'm through with Newlin,' replied Johnny.

He was about ready to leave the doctor's when there was a knock on the door and when the doctor returned he brought with him a girl from the saloon.

'Durango,' he said. 'Margie says she wants a word with you.'

'I was in the saloon just now and saw you with Ruth. No one knows I've come out so I daren't be away very long but I desperately want a word with you.' Margie looked anxiously at the doctor.

He smiled. 'All right,' he said, 'I'll go into the other room; give me a shout when you're leavin'!'

As the door closed behind him Margie swung round to face Johnny. 'After I heard you mention Nick Sheridan's death, I concluded that was what you had been talking to Ruth about.'

'That's right,' agreed Johnny. 'But what has it to do with you?'

'I always thought there was something queer that night,' she went on quickly. 'Ruth had taken Nick upstairs and a short while later I went up to the adjoining room – Curt used to let us use it if we wanted a break. The walls are fairly thin and when Ruth gets into a temper she talks rather loudly. Sheridan seemed to be awkward about telling her something but eventually she must have got what she wanted because things quietened down.'

'What did Nick tell her?' asked Johnny eagerly.

'I don't know,' replied Margie, 'I couldn't hear what he said.'

'Anything happen after that?' queried Johnny.

'I was about to return to the saloon,' explained Margie, 'when I heard Ruth leaving the room. I waited with the door ajar and saw her go to Curt Simpson's room. A few minutes later she returned and took Nick back to the bar. I hurried downstairs and a short while later Curt came down and spoke to his two side-kicks – the two you've just killed. When Nick left a short while afterwards they went out too. When they returned they went straight to see Curt.'

'So you reckon they killed Nick on Curt's instructions, after Ruth had got certain information from Nick,' said Johnny excitedly.

'I'm not saying anything like that; I don't know,' said Margie. 'I'm only telling you what happened, something that wasn't mentioned at the inquest.'

'Why are you tellin' me all this?' asked Johnny.

Margie smiled warmly. 'Let's say I don't like Ruth and Curt Simpson doesn't treat me like he used to,' she said. 'I must get back.' She turned to the door but Johnny stopped her.

'Thanks for coming,' he said. 'Just two more questions. Did Nick drink a lot that night?'

'Nothing exceptional,' came the reply, 'but Ruth has been known to slip something into men's drinks.'

Johnny nodded. 'Do you know if Simpson is involved in any of the land deals?'

The surprised look which came on Margie's face was not lost on Johnny. 'I shouldn't think so,' she replied. 'He's a town man and the Gay Lady is his pride and joy. Now I must go.'

Johnny thanked her again and the girl hurried away from the doctor's house.

Ten minutes later it was a thoughtful Johnny Durango who strolled into the bank to see the manager.

'I hear there was a bit of trouble in the Gay Lady,' said Mike Hardy. 'How's the arm?'

'Nothing to worry; the Doc's patched it up. I'm sorry to bother you again but I think I might be on to something which might show that Nick Sheridan didn't commit suicide.'

'Anything I can do to help if you can prove that?' said the manager.

'Would you say Curt Simpson was interested in buying land?' asked Johnny.

'I wouldn't think so,' replied Mike. 'I suppose I shouldn't tell you this but his account has had no large withdrawals since he extended the Gay Lady. If you think he's behind these land deals I think you're mistaken. The money for those was put into a special account and our lawyer, Luke Ashton, had the power to use it when a deal was completed.'

'Where did that money come from?' questioned Johnny.

'Several places,' replied Hardy. 'It was transferred from a number of banks in the east and a couple in New Mexico.'

Johnny's thoughts raced but he did not voice them to Hardy. Instead he asked for a loan of five hundred dollars.

When the bank manager had arranged this Johnny made his way to the Gay Lady. When he swung through the doors the occupants of the saloon were so surprised that a silence descended quickly. Heads turned to watch this young cowboy who had only a short while ago outshot two men. Sheriff Mart Webster, who was still at the bar, turned and, leaning with his back to the long counter, watched Johnny through cold eyes. Johnny crossed the room, hurried up the stairs, rapped sharply on the door of Curt Simpson's room and walked in.

The saloon owner looked up annoyed that someone should burst in before he had acknowledged their knock. When he saw Johnny Durango anger welled up inside him; his eyes narrowed with hate.

'What do you want?' he snarled.

Johnny slammed the door behind him. 'When you set two of your side-kicks on me make sure they're better men,' he rapped, 'maybe you put Blackie Farrow to get me, maybe it was you who set three men to beat me up and tried to have me killed by a supposedly uncontrollable horse.' Protestations rose to Curt Simpson's lips but were halted as Johnny went on. 'Why do you want Johnny Durango out of the way? What are you frightened he might find out? The truth about Nick Sheridan's death? Maybe it was those two men who died today who killed him but they are the type who only obey orders; did you give those orders, Simpson?'

As Johnny's words lashed around his head Curt Simpson's face grew dark with anger. His knuckles showed white as he clenched his hands tightly, fighting to keep control of himself. How much did this man know? Or was it all guess work?

'I don't know what you're talking about, Durango,' hissed Simpson. 'You get out of here. You heard what the sheriff told you and...'

Johnny smiled. He had to admire the way Simpson had not risen to his taunts and yet in that fact Johnny felt the big man had something to hide and did not want to be drawn. Any man to whom these words had been directed would have hit out if he had nothing to hide.

'All right, Simpson,' interrupted Johnny. 'Just settle one thing for me. You said you held IOUs for five hundred dollars from Nick Sheridan; I'll redeem them.'

'I'll only do that with Mrs Sheridan,' hissed Simpson.

Johnny's Colt sprang to his hand. 'You do it with me,' he snapped. 'Now, get them!'

Simpson hesitated a moment then moved slowly round his desk. He opened a drawer, pulled out two slips of paper and tossed them on to the desk. Johnny stepped forward, picked them up and glanced casually at them.

'Thank you,' he grinned. He holstered his gun and threw the five hundred dollars to Simpson. He picked up a match from the desk, set fire to the IOUs, let them drop on the desk and watched the flames flare and die leaving the ashes curling.

Johnny touched them with his finger and they disintegrated. He smiled at Simpson's angry face, spun on his heel and walked to the door. He paused with his hand on the knob and looked back at the saloon owner.

'Too bad you won't be able to use them to force Mrs Sheridan's hand to sell the Three Rs,' he said then swung out of the room and, without a glance at anyone, left the Gay Lady.

# SIX

Dan Neale was having breakfast with his wife when the sound of a hard ridden horse brought Dan to his feet. He strapped on his gun-belt quickly and took down a rifle from the rack on the wall.

'Be careful, Dan,' pleaded his wife, alarm showing on her face and in her voice.

'I'll be all right, Stella,' answered Dan as he strode to the door. 'It may be nothing, but someone's in a hurry.' He flung open the door and stepped out on to the veranda to see a horseman approaching from the direction of town. 'It's Vernon Petch,' he called over his shoulder and a moment later his wife joined him.

The rider slowed his horse as he neared the house and pulled up close to the veranda.

'Howdy, Vernon,' greeted Dan, 'what brings you out here so early?'

'I've got to speak to you,' replied Petch breathing deeply after the fast ride.

'Come along inside,' said Dan. 'Have a

cup of coffee, we're just finishing breakfast.'

'Thanks,' said Vernon and swinging from the saddle followed Stella and Dan into the house. The thin, pale-faced man took off his low-crowned sombrero and sat down at the table with the Neales.

'You were ridin' hard and we don't often see you this way,' remarked Dan. 'What's worryin' you?' Dan could tell from the look in Petch's eyes and nervous way in which he twitched his long boney fingers that something was wrong.

'Have you heard about the shootin' in the Gay Lady, yesterday?' asked Petch.

'No,' replied Dan. 'Who was it?' he added, his thoughts flying to Johnny.

Petch went on to relate the happenings in the saloon and Dan listened without speaking. 'It was a remark this fellow Durango made that's brought me out here,' he added at the conclusion of his story.

Dan looked at him curiously. 'What was that?' he asked.

'Durango told the sheriff he might be asking him to re-open the case of Nick Sheridan's death,' explained Petch. 'I didn't think much about it at the time but I was telling Emily about it over breakfast this morning; my son Ken was there and told me he knew that Nick did not kill himself.'

'What!' Dan and Stella gasped together looking at Petch wide-eyed with surprise.

'Why didn't he say anything before?' asked Dan.

'Well he's only fourteen,' said Vernon. 'He saw the actual killing and that scared him. He said nothing to me nor to his mother until this morning when he blurted it out after I had told Emily what Durango had said.'

'Then he knows who did it?' said Dan.

'Those two side-kicks of Curt Simpson's Durango shot yesterday and a third man whom Ken didn't know,' answered Petch. 'I went to see the sheriff but he wasn't in. I tried to find Durango but he's not in town, so knowing you and Nick were great friends, I thought I'd tell you. I figured that if this Durango was interested in Nick Sheridan you might know him.'

'I sure do!' cried Dan excitedly as he jumped up from his chair. 'And we're ridin' to see him now.'

Vernon Petch gulped down his coffee and quickly followed Dan outside. The two men were soon heading for the Three Rs at a fast pace.

After his interview with Curt Simpson Johnny Durango returned to the Three Rs having decided to await developments. He figured that he had stirred things up enough for someone to get curious about how much he knew and he hoped that by forcing the action he would get a lead on the mystery behind Nick Sheridan's death.

Kathy was concerned when she saw his bandaged arm and again wondered if it would be better to sell and leave the district. The Three Rs cowboys were briefed to look out for trouble but the latest development came from an unexpected quarter when, the following morning Johnny saw Dan Neale galloping towards the ranch with a stranger.

Johnny was sitting on the corral fence when the two men pulled up in front of him.

'Johnny, I want you to meet Vernon Petch,' said Dan after he and Johnny had exchanged greetings. 'Vernon, Johnny Durango.'

'Pleased to know you,' called Petch.

'Howdy,' greeted Johnny eyeing the man whom he judged to be about forty-five.

'Vernon has something mighty important to tell you but I think Kathy had better hear it as well.'

'She's in the house,' said Johnny, jumping down from the fence. 'Come on over.'

The two men swung from their saddles and walked with Durango towards the house. Kathy, who had seen them approaching, came on to the veranda to meet them. She was surprised to see Vernon Petch, for he was a man who had lived in Newlin for twenty years and was hardly ever seen on the back of a horse. Kathy led the way into the room and, when they were all seated, Dan told Vernon to tell Kathy and Johnny exactly what he had told him.

'We were right all along,' said Johnny excitedly. 'Nick didn't commit suicide.'

There were tears in Kathy's eyes. 'This fits in with what Margie told you,' she said. 'I thought Nick must have been got at to do the things they said he'd done, now after what she told you and what Vernon has said … well…' The words choked in her throat.

'Your faith in Nick has always been there,' comforted Dan. 'We're a step nearer getting the person behind it all.'

'It seems you got two of the killers, yesterday,' said Petch. 'As slick a bit of shootin' as I've ever seen.'

'Margie didn't mention a third man leaving the Gay lady that night,' mused Johnny. 'I wonder if it could have been the third man that beat me up.' He turned to Petch.

'I'd like to see your son,' he said.

'Right,' answered Petch. 'I left him at home with his mother.'

The three men were soon riding for Newlin and as they neared the town, Petch headed for a neat house on the edge of town. It was well kept, the garden well tended and a newly whitened fence surrounded the Petch property. Vernon led the way into the house and, as he crossed the hall, called to his wife but there was no reply. The house seemed to greet the shout with a mocking silence, and Johnny sensed something was wrong. Petch, a look of concern on his face, threw open the kitchen door.

'Emily!' he gasped and leaped forward to his wife who was gagged and bound to a chair.

Johnny and Dan hastened to help him unbind his wife.

'What happened?' asked Vernon anxiously.

'Oh, Vernon, I thought you'd never come,' sobbed his wife. 'They've taken Ken!'

'What!' Amazement crossed Vernon's face.

'Who did it, Mrs Petch?' asked Johnny.

She shook her head. 'I don't know,' she went on. 'There was a knock on the back door and when I answered it two masked men forced their way in at the point of a gun. They bound and gagged me and took Ken away.'

'You didn't recognize them?' asked Dan.

'No,' replied Mrs Petch, 'but I did notice one of them had a scar above his left eyebrow.'

'You're sure it was the left eyebrow?' Johnny asked excitedly.

'Certain,' came the reply.

'One of the men who beat me up had the same mark,' went on Johnny. 'This is obviously a plan to stop Ken from talking. He's the only witness to Nick's murder; but what puzzles me is how did they know Ken had seen it happen.' He looked at Vernon Petch. 'You told no one else about this before going to see Dan?' he asked.

Petch shook his head. 'No one,' he answered. 'Naturally I went to the sheriff first but he wasn't in.'

'The sheriff!' Johnny gasped. 'Did you leave a message for him with anyone?'

'I left a note on his desk,' replied Vernon.

'What did it say?' asked Johnny.

'I merely mentioned that Ken had some vital information regarding Sheridan's death and would he come round to see me as soon as he got in?'

'And he never came?' Johnny put the

query to Mrs Sheridan.

'No,' she replied.

Then I reckon we'd better pay that lawman a visit,' said Johnny.

After they had made sure that Mrs Sheridan was all right the three men hurried to the sheriff's office. They found him seated behind his desk studying some 'Wanted' posters. He looked up with surprise when the door was flung open and the three men strode in. His eyes narrowed when he saw Johnny Durango.

'You're bent on ignoring my advice,' he said. 'I suppose trouble's following you again.'

'It sure is, sheriff,' replied Johnny tensely, 'and this time it's right in your lap.'

'I didn't know you two were cronies of Durango,' observed the sheriff glancing at the other two men.

Dan grinned and ignored the remark. 'Tell Mart what has happened, Vernon,' he said.

Petch related the information as given to him by his son. At Johnny's request he was careful not to mention the kidnapping. The sheriff's eyes widened as he listened to the story.

'Wal, it seems a lot of people were wrong about Sheridan's death,' he said. 'It's a pity

Ken didn't come forward before. Did he recognize these men?'

'Two were the men killed in the saloon yesterday,' put in Johnny, 'but the third he didn't know.'

The sheriff looked thoughtful. Suddenly he snapped his fingers. 'Blackie Farrow,' he said. 'The killer must have been a stranger for Ken not to recognize him so Blackie Farrow is a possibility.'

'You could be right,' replied Johnny. 'A hired killer operating with two of Curt Simpson's side-kicks – may be Simpson knows more about this matter than it appears.'

'Now wait a minute,' protested the sheriff, 'you just can't...'

'Hold on, Webster,' put in Johnny, 'You haven't heard it all yet. Ken's been kidnapped.'

'What!' gasped the sheriff.

'An' I reckon you might know something,' went on Johnny hotly.

The sheriff sprang to his feet. 'See here, Durango, I'm about fed up with you!' he shouted.

Johnny ignored the lawman. He stormed on. 'As soon as Ken told his father about Nick's death, Vernon naturally came straight to you. You weren't in so he left a note and decided that as Dan was a close friend of Nick's he would ride to see him. They came to see me and when we got back to town Ken had gone, kidnapped by two hombres. The only other person to know apart from us was you!'

As the implication of these words hit Vernon Petch he stared in amazement at the sheriff. Suddenly he leaped forward grasping the sheriff by the shirt.

'Why you...' he screamed. 'Where's my boy? If you've harmed him I'll...'

Johnny and Dan jumped forward pulling Petch off the sheriff.

'Ease off, Vernon!' cried Dan. 'We haven't got any proof that Mart's in on this.'

Anger flowed from the lawman's face. 'You're darned right you haven't!' he stormed. 'I've good a mind to clamp you in jail!' His voice eased a little and he looked hard at Johnny who thought he had detected a look of alarm cross the sheriff's eyes at the implication. 'There's something you've forgotten,' he went on, 'Petch left a note here, anyone could have come in and seen it.'

'That's right, Johnny,' agreed Dan realizing the sheriff would not be drawn and that Durango had gone far enough at the moment.

'Well, what are you goin' to do about it?'

asked Petch.

'I'll raise a posse an' we'll make a search,' answered Webster. 'But we've little to go on. Did your wife see these men?'

'They were masked,' explained Petch, 'but one had a scar over his left eyebrow.'

The sheriff shrugged his shoulders. 'I'll do my best,' he said. 'I think you'd better go back home.'

'Mind if Dan and I ride with you?' asked Johnny watching Webster carefully.

'No,' replied the sheriff coldly. He looked hard at Johnny. 'But no trouble from you. Be ready in half an hour.'

The three men left the sheriff's office and returned to Vernon's house to find that, although Mrs Petch was naturally worried, she had got over the initial shock. She soon had the men some coffee ready.

'It's a nice place you've got here,' observed Johnny as he sipped his coffee.

'We were very fortunate,' replied Vernon. 'I had a store in town, did quite well but then Curt Simpson made me a big offer for it. It was too good a chance to miss so we took it.'

Johnny looked up an expression of curious surprise on his face. 'Curt Simpson? Is he in the store business as well?'

Petch smiled. 'No,' he replied, 'but my

property adjoined the Gay Lady and he wanted to extend. Can't understand why, the saloon was big enough as it was but this – anyone would think Newlin was a booming mining town.'

'Simpson's eccentricities,' said Dan.

'I wonder,' mused Johnny. 'He keeps coming into this whole affair but I can't help feeling there's someone bigger behind it all. However, I reckon things have been stirred up and if we keep our eyes open whoever it is may make a move. I figure there's three people we've got to watch. Simpson, Webster and Amos North.'

Petch was somewhat puzzled by this last remark and Dan and Johnny quickly filled him in on what had happened.

'The important thing at the moment,' concluded Johnny, 'is to find Ken. He's the only witness.'

'You don't think they'll kill him!' cried Mrs Petch in alarm.

Vernon put a comforting arm round his wife. 'They wouldn't kill a boy,' he said, but his own thoughts doubted that statement.

Johnny and Dan picked up their sombreros and crossed to the door where Johnny hesitated.

'Anything else you think might help us,

Mrs Petch?' he asked.

'Only that I thought they rode off in a westerly direction,' she replied.

Johnny and Dan left the house and joined the posse which had gathered in front of the sheriff's office.

'We'll split into two groups,' called out Webster. 'Half of you go with my deputy and work to the east and circle back from the north. The rest come with me; we'll head west and swing south.'

'Mrs Petch thought the kidnappers rode off in a westerly direction,' shouted Johnny.

The sheriff stiffened in his saddle. 'I'm runnin' this show, Durango. Those men could have circled so we'll do it my way.'

Johnny looked at Dan. 'You ride with the deputy, I'll keep an eye on the lawman. See you back at Vernon Petch's.'

Dan nodded and a few minutes later two groups of riders headed away from Newlin in opposite directions.

The sun was low in the western sky when they returned, tired and hungry after a long day in the saddle. The sheriff and Johnny rode to the Petch's house and found that Dan had already arrived.

'I'm sorry,' said the sheriff to the parents, anxiously awaiting news, 'but we drew a blank. Not a trace at all.'

Mrs Petch looked despondent at the news but she put on a brave face.

'I know you've all done your best,' she said. 'You've had a wearying day; I've got a meal ready; you must stay and have some.'

In spite of their protests Emily Petch insisted and soon the men were enjoying a tasty meal. They were having some coffee when they heard the pound of a hard ridden horse approaching. It began to slow as it neared the house and they looked at each other, wondering who the rider was that came out of the night. The horse stopped, then there was a shattering of glass as a stone hurtled through the window and clattered on to the floor. At the same time there was the sound of the horse being pushed into a gallop as the rider urged it away into the safety of the darkness. The four men in the house leaped towards the door. Johnny was first to reach it and he ran outside, his gun already in his hand. His eyes pierced the darkness but there was nothing to see and only the pound of vanishing hoofs signified the path of the rider. Johnny raised his Colt and fired three shots in the direction of the sound but the noise never faltered and seemed to mock Johnny's hopeless attempt to stop the horseman. Dan moved towards his horse.

'It's no use, Dan,' cried Johnny, 'our horses are tired after that riding today. We'd never catch him.'

Reluctantly Dan had to admit he was right and the four men filed back into the house to find Mrs Petch reading a piece of paper which she had just unfastened from the stone.

'What is it, Emily?' asked Vernon moving to his wife's side.

She handed him the paper. 'What are we going to do?' she asked. There was a pleading note in her voice, as if begging her husband to find an answer.

He stared at the note then read it aloud slowly. 'Your son is safe. Leave three thousand dollars in the old shack on the west trail at six tomorrow night and your son will be returned.'

'Here let me see that,' said the sheriff, taking the piece of paper from Petch. There was a note of surprise tinged with alarm in his voice which did not go unnoticed by Johnny.

'We must do as it says, Vernon,' cried Mrs Petch.

'It will take all our money,' said her husband. 'Just when we've got nicely settled, but, if it means getting Ken back, we'll do it.'

The sheriff glanced up from the note which he had been studying. 'Wal, it looks like a simple case of kidnapping,' he said, 'and not because he knew who killed Sheridan. There's one thing, we know he's alive. Don't worry, Mrs Petch, we'll get him safely back to you. Don't do anything until I see you tomorrow, in the meantime I'll take this note and see if I can find anyone who recognizes the writing.'

Johnny was preoccupied with his thoughts as Mart Webster gathered up his sombrero and left the house but as soon as he was gone he spoke quickly and urgently.

'I don't believe it is a straight-forward case of kidnapping for money,' he said. 'I believe it had something to do with the fact that Ken saw the killing an' I reckon the sheriff knows more about it than he makes out. I feel sure he's linked with Curt Simpson in this. Come on, Dan, we'll follow him.'

The two men hurried from the house and saw the sheriff riding down the main street. They hurried along the roadway keeping him in sight and when they saw him pull up outside the Gay Lady they quickened their step. When Webster disappeared inside the saloon the two men broke into a run and, as they stepped quietly inside the door, they saw the sheriff hurrying along the balcony! He knocked on the door and disappeared into Curt Simpson's room.

'He's come straight to Simpson,' whispered Johnny. 'He was a bit scared when he heard Vernon read that note. I'd love to know what's being said in there now.'

'What are we goin' to do?' asked Dan as they stepped outside again.

'I'm not sure,' replied Johnny thoughtfully. 'We must be very careful; we want Ken alive and I have a feeling that his life might be in great danger after what happened tonight. I think something has gone wrong with the plans. Somehow or other we've got to keep an eye on any movements that come via Curt Simpson.'

Dan looked thoughtful. 'I've been trying to put myself in the place of a kidnapper and I reckon if I wanted to hide out I'd choose the Palo Duro Canyon. Did you search that way today?'

'Webster wouldn't go down it,' replied Johnny, 'said there were so many hiding places it would take too long. We rode along the rim for a good way but saw nothing.'

'Maybe it fits in with the old shack they chose for the deposit of the ransom money,' went on Dan. 'It stands on the west trail close to a fork where an old track leads to the Canyon. It would be a convenient place if they are hiding out there.'

'Then if Simpson is behind this he is going to contact them or send someone else to do it. Would they head that way into the Canyon?' asked Johnny.

'I reckon so,' replied Dan.

'Then I think the only thing to do is to play a hunch,' said Johnny. 'If we hang around here anyone could leave town without us knowing, so I think the best thing is to hide out in that hut; if anyone takes the old trail I'll know.'

'Let's go then,' said Dan.

'Not you,' answered Johnny and stopped any protestations that sprang to Dan's lips. 'Your wife will be worried stiff about you. I figure you'd better get home.'

'I'd feel easier if I was with you, you may need some help,' said Dan.

'I'll be all right,' replied Johnny, 'besides one man can often tail others better than two.'

Johnny would hear no more about it and they returned to see Vernon Petch from whom Johnny borrowed a fresh horse and whilst Dan headed for the Circle A, Johnny rode to keep a lonely vigil in an old shack.

# SEVEN

When Mart Webster entered Curt Simpson's room the saloon owner greeted him with a smile.

'Howdy, Mart,' he said. 'I hope you led those nosey-parkers a dance today.'

'Sure did,' replied the sheriff. 'I kept them out of Palo Duro Canyon but there's something going on down there I don't like.'

Simpson's smile vanished when he saw the serious expression on Webster's face.

'What do you mean?' he asked.

'I went to Petch's place when we got back, Durango and Neale were there as well. Mrs Petch gave us a meal and whilst we were having it a stone with a note attached was thrown through the window. It was a ransom note demanding three thousand dollars for the return of Ken Petch.'

'What!' Simpson gasped. His face darkened with anger. 'The double-crossing coyotes! I picked Langley and Dixon thinking I could trust them. I told them to hold the boy until I sent them word. The boss is due tomorrow and I figured he could decide what to do with him.'

'I don't think I'll be able to stall the Petch's from paying,' said Webster, 'not the way Mrs Petch feels.'

'I reckon we'll have to deal with those two double-crossers and the boy at the same time,' said Simpson. He looked thoughtful. 'Whoever threw that stone wouldn't know you were there so they won't know that we're on to them. I'll send Raven and Dale to the Palo Duro tomorrow to deal with Langley, Dixon and the boy.'

'What about Durango?' asked Webster.

'So far it's all guesswork with him,' replied Curt. 'But something will have to be done about him; his guesses are getting pretty near the mark. He now has what he wanted – definite evidence that Sheridan was murdered – but he can't connect us with it. I'll see what the boss suggests about him; Durango seems to bear a charmed life.'

The two men talked about an hour before Webster left the Gay Lady, but they would not have been so easy in their minds if they had known that Johnny Durango was riding towards a lonely hut.

Although it was dark, Johnny found the hut without much difficulty. He figured that if any contact was to be made with the kidnappers it would be done in daylight because the Palo Duro Canyon was no place to be moving through in the dark. Nevertheless Johnny kept watch for over an hour, but as nothing moved in the silent Texas night, he decided he could bed down. In spite of the wearying day in the saddle Johnny slept lightly and was awake before sun-up. As the sun broke the eastern horizon he moved away from the hut and sought the cover of some rocks a short distance from the trail. After securing his horse he made himself comfortable and awaited developments, hoping that his hunch would prove correct. If not he feared no one would see Ken Petch alive again.

He had been waiting an hour when suddenly he stiffened. He inclined his head, listening intently. The faint sound of distant hoof-beats reached his ears. Johnny eased himself amongst the rocks and, searching the landscape in the direction of Newlin, he saw two riders. Excitement seized him. Were these the men he expected? Would they turn off the trail and head for the Palo Duro Canyon? The men were riding at a fast pace and were soon approaching the fork. Johnny tensed himself then relief swept over him when, without hesitation, the two men left the trail and took the old track towards the Canyon. Although he could not be certain, he felt sure that he and Dan had figured correctly.

He studied the men carefully and even though he did not know them he had a feeling that he had seen them in the Gay Lady. Once they were past his hiding place he slipped quickly to his horse, swung into the saddle and followed them, using every available cover whilst keeping as close as he dare. Whatever happened he must not slip up now.

When they reached the edge of the Canyon the two men pulled to a halt and seemed to be having a discussion. Johnny smiled to himself when, a few minutes later, they climbed from their saddles. He reckoned they did not want the kidnappers to know of their approach and had figured it better to go the rest of the way on foot in case the sound of horses' hoofs betrayed them. This suited Johnny because now he could keep really close to the two men. He slipped from the saddle and when they disappeared over the rim of the Canyon he hurried forward to drop flat on his stomach to peer into the Palo Duro.

The sides of the Canyon were rugged and steep, dropping almost a thousand feet to the Red River, but Johnny saw that a short distance to his right, there were a series of wide shelves along the wall of rock. At that point the side of the Canyon was less sheer and the two men were making their way along the path towards it. Johnny kept to the side of the path, using boulders and outcrops of rock to cover him. When the path widened on to one of the shelves the two men hurried forward to the cliff face which projected across the shelves. They edged their way round it on a path only wide enough for a horse to use. Once they were out of sight Johnny ran forward and, moving cautiously round the projecting cliff, saw that the path led on to a continuation of the wide shelf. Johnny tensed himself when he saw the two men moving from boulder to boulder towards an old dilapidated hut standing a short distance away close to the cliff face.

When they were twenty yards away from the hut the two men stopped and drew their Colts. Durango gasped when he realized the meaning of their action. No one was going to come out of that hut alive! This was to be the pay off for the double-crossers and Ken

Petch would never return to Newlin to tell his story. Johnny drew his Colt and moved quickly forward closing the gap between himself and the two men.

The would-be assassins, using cover, moved to the side of the hut which had no window and then crept stealthily towards the door. In the mean-time Johnny had moved forward directly towards the door and was now crouching behind a boulder not ten yards away. When the men reached the door Johnny sprang from his cover.

'Hold it!' he yelled.

Surprised by this unexpected shout the two men spun round, their Colts swinging upwards, but seeing their intention Johnny was already squeezing the trigger. The bullet took the first man high on the chest sending him staggering backwards. Almost as soon as he fired Johnny dived forward and the shot from the second man whined over his head. Johnny fired again before the man could take a new line on him and he saw the man grasp at his stomach, double up, and pitch forward to lie still in a heap.

Astonished by the sudden roar of guns the two men in the hut grabbed their Colts and leaped to the door. As they flung it open they saw Johnny, a smoking Colt in his hand, lying a few yards away. A third bullet ripped from Johnny's gun and one of the men pitched forward to lie lifeless on the ground. The remaining man slammed the door. Johnny realized there was not a moment to lose. He must not give the remaining man time to use Ken as a protection. Johnny leaped to his feet, raced the few yards to the hut and flung himself at the door which burst open with a crash. As he fell into the hut he was aware of a figure beside the door. He rolled over; there was a roar as the man fired and the bullet whined close to Johnny's ear. Durango squeezed the trigger of his Colt and saw the man jerk upright. The frightened expression on the man's face changed to one of surprise. He tried to bring his gun to bear on Johnny but the strength seemed to have gone out of his arm. He staggered against the wall and slid slowly to the floor.

As Johnny pushed himself to his feet he was aware of a frightened boy standing against the opposite wall.

'It's all right, Ken,' he said, his voice quiet and friendly. 'It's all over, I'm taking you back to your mother.'

The boy stared wide-eyed at the stranger, but when he saw the warm smile on Johnny's face he rushed forward flinging his arms round Johnny's waist pressing his head hard against the man's chest. Johnny slipped his Colt back into his holster and placed a strong comforting arm round Ken's shoulders.

'We'll soon have you home, son and there'll be no more trouble for you,' said Johnny.

The boy looked up and a faint smile flickered his lips. Johnny turned and led the boy outside. Before long they were clambering back up the side of the Canyon and, when they reached the top, Johnny collected one of the dead men's horses for Ken and soon they were heading back to Newlin.

Before they pulled to a halt outside the house the door burst open and Mrs Petch ran down the path. There were tears in her eyes as she flung her arms round her son almost before he had time to jump down from the horse's back. Mrs Petch looked at Johnny and in that look he saw all the gratitude that would be difficult for her to put into words.

'We'll never be out of your debt, Durango,' said Vernon Petch, shaking Johnny firmly by the hand. 'Where did you find him?'

'In the Palo Duro Canyon,' replied Johnny. 'There's quite a story to it and I reckon the sheriff had better hear it too,' he added seeing Mart Webster standing in the doorway of the house.

'Come along inside,' said Vernon and the two men followed Mrs Petch and Ken along the path.

'Congratulations, Durango,' praised Mart Webster hiding his real feeling behind an impassive face.

Mrs Petch soon had some coffee ready and as they enjoyed it Johnny told his story, saying that he had been riding near the Canyon when he had seen two horsemen and had followed them. He did not reveal his suspicions of Curt Simpson and the sheriff. When he finished he looked at Ken. 'Do you think you could tell the sheriff and myself what you saw on the night of Mr Sheridan's death?'

The boy nodded. 'I was on my way home from my aunty's and was cutting through the alley next to the saloon when three men came round the corner, pushing Mr Sheridan in front of them. Mr Sheridan seemed to be drunk and he fell to the ground. As he lay there one of the men shot him and then left. The other two seemed to check things over, then one of them took Mr Sheridan's gun and fired one shot into the air. He then put the gun into Mr Sheridan's hand and they both went away.'

Johnny looked at the sheriff. 'I think that is sufficient to prove Nick did not commit suicide.'

The lawman agreed. 'Did you know any of these men?' he asked Ken.

Ken described the two men whom Johnny had killed in the saloon and the description of the third fitted Blackie Farrow.

'Wal,' said the sheriff looking at Johnny when Ken had finished. 'It seems you've already accounted for the killers, so that puts an end to that.'

Johnny did not speak as the sheriff pushed himself to his feet. This might be the end as far as the law was concerned but as for Johnny Durango he knew there was something much bigger behind the death of Nick Sheridan and he was determined to find out what it was. When the sheriff had left the house Johnny turned to Mr and Mrs Petch.

'I don't want to worry Ken unduly,' he said, 'but I would like to ask him another question.'

'Well, he needs a good sleep to get over–' began Mrs Petch a natural concern in her voice.

'Emily,' interrupted her husband. 'Johnny saved our son. If we can help him in any way

I think we should.'

'Thank you,' said Johnny. 'It will only take a minute. The sheriff was only interested in a description of the men who killed Nick and because those men are dead he thinks that's an end to the matter; now I don't, because I think there is much more behind it, otherwise why bother to kidnap Ken?'

'But the ransom demand,' said Mrs Petch, 'surely that means...'

'I don't think so,' broke in Johnny, 'I believe that was just a case of thieves falling out. Someone tried to be smart and tried to cash in on this business.' He turned to the boy. 'Ken,' he said, 'the third man you described was the man who tried to kill me on my way to Newlin; I wondered if you had seen him before or after Mr Sheridan was killed.'

The boy looked thoughtful. 'Dad sometimes lets me go out riding; there's a little gully in the hills, north of Mr Sheridan's spread, with a stream running through it, that I liked to go to. Two days after Mr Sheridan was killed, I went up there. I was about to ride into the gully when I saw two men; one of them was the man I described.'

'Did they see you?' asked Johnny.

'No,' replied the boy with a shake of his

head. 'I kept out of sight until they had gone.'

'Who was he with?' asked Johnny.

'Mr Simpson, the saloon owner,' answered Ken.

His mother and father gasped. 'What does all this mean?' asked Vernon.

Johnny's eyes were bright with excitement. 'I don't know yet,' he replied. 'But I think we are goin' to find Curt Simpson is somewhere behind Nick Sheridan's death.' He picked up his Stetson. 'Thanks for all the help, Ken,' he said.

'I think it's you we have to thank,' said Vernon as Johnny left the house.

Durango swung into the saddle and turned his horse along the west road from town, unaware that he was being followed by Sheriff Mart Webster.

When he left the house the sheriff waited further along the street keeping watch for Johnny leaving. He had been taken by surprise when Johnny had turned up with Ken. Somehow the cowboy had got to know about Simpson's plan to kill the boy, but how, Webster could not understand. He felt that, although the killers of Nick Sheridan had been accounted for, Durango was not satisfied. Webster knew he must tell Simpson what had happened as soon as possible and yet he did not want to have Durango moving around without knowing what he was up to. Curt Simpson would have to wait for the news; this man Durango needed watching.

The sheriff matched his pace to that of the man ahead, and for some reason he was not surprised when he realized Durango was heading for Dan Neale's spread.

The back of the house was sheltered from the winds by a hillock which was strewn with rocks and boulders and the sheriff found it an easy matter after leaving his horse out of sight to approach the house unseen. When still a short distance away Webster paused and surveyed the ranch below him. There was no sign of life and he guessed the hired hands must be out on the range. When Durango disappeared from view round the front of the house, Webster moved forward quickly until he was close to the back of the house. He could see Mrs Neale through a window and he hoped that Johnny's arrival would take her out of the room. A moment later he was glad to see her disappear and he glided swiftly forward to the timber wall of the house. Inching his way to the corner he peered round cautiously and after checking that no one was in sight he turned along the side of the house. A few paces on he froze in his tracks. Voices drifted to him and excitement seized him when he realized they came from an open window. He edged his way nearer until he was able to distinguish the words. Johnny had just started to tell the Neales about the recovery of Ken Petch.

'It's a good job we followed Webster after the Petch's got that ransom note,' said Dan Neale, 'and then played the hunch that Simpson was behind the kidnapping and would do something about it.'

Mart Webster stiffened. His thoughts raced; now he knew how Durango had got on to the kidnappers, guesswork had turned out to be right.

'Another point,' said Johnny, 'Ken saw Curt Simpson and Blackie Farrow together.'

'Then it is Simpson who is behind it all,' exclaimed Dan.

'I'm still not sure about that,' replied Johnny. 'From what I gather about Simpson he's hardly the type to go in for land buying, besides from the look of the Gay Lady he's sunk a lot of money there.'

'Can't think why he made the place so much bigger,' mused Dan. 'You'd almost think he was expecting a big influx of people around here and yet I can't see how that could happen.'

'I'm told that these offers have been coming from back East,' said Johnny, 'for someone acting through Newlin's lawyer. The only link I can find with the East is the fact that Amos North has land near Fort Worth. Do you know anything about him, Dan?'

'I'm afraid not,' answered Dan. 'He's very seldom here from all accounts and I've never met him.'

'That bears out what Kathy told me,' answered Johnny. 'I think I'll take a ride out that way and look his place over, see if I can learn anything.'

'I'd come with you, Johnny,' said Dan, 'but I'm hoping to put through a land deal this evening. What I tell you is in strict confidence. I don't want this to get out until the deal is through. The spread to the west of here is owned by Wes Jenkins but it is not generally known that he owns a two mile strip between my spread and the hills to the north.'

'In other words it is between your ranch and that belonging to Amos North,' said Johnny.

'That's right,' answered Dan. 'As a matter of fact when Luke Ashton came with his offer to buy my spread he had included that stretch belonging to Wes Jenkins. I didn't enlighten him that it wasn't mine as I hoped to get it. Jenkins does nothing with it and is willing to sell and I'm hoping to complete the deal tonight.'

'Best of luck,' said Johnny. 'I'll let you know if I learn anything after my visit to the Twisted F, but first I must go back to the Three Rs; Kathy will be wondering what has become of me.'

Realizing Johnny Durango was about to leave, Mart Webster, excited by the information he gained, slipped away from the house to the cover of the boulders on the hillock. He moved quickly to the top from where he watched Durango leave the Circle A and ride in the direction of the Three Rs. Webster hurried to his horse and sent it into a fast gallop towards Newlin.

The sheriff hit the town at a hard pace but did not slow down until he neared the Gay Lady. He was out of the saddle almost before the horse had stopped. Slinging the reins over the rail he hurried inside and took the stairs two at a time. Curt Simpson looked up in surprise when his door burst open and Mart Webster strode in banging the door behind him.

'What's wrong with you?' asked Simpson noting the serious face of the dust-covered, panting lawman.

'Durango rescued Ken Petch,' gasped Webster.

'What!' Simpson was taken aback at this news. 'But how could he?'

Webster went on to relate the facts as he knew them and then told Simpson what he had overheard at the Circle A.

Simpson was a very thoughtful man by the time Webster had finished his story. He puffed hard at a cheroot and paced the floor, his face dark with annoyance at the turn of events.

'We've got to act now, and act quickly,' he said. 'If Durango gets out to the Twisted F and finds out anything about Amos North everything will be ruined. I reckon we'd better ride out and see North; I think he will have arrived. We can then arrange a little reception for Durango.'

Before long the two men were riding north from Newlin in the direction of the hills and the Twisted F spread.

Kathy Sheridan was so relieved to see Johnny approaching the Three Rs that she hurried from the house to meet him.

'I'm so glad you're back,' she said. 'I was

worried when you did not come back last night.'

Johnny swung from the saddle. He smiled at Kathy's concern. 'I'm all right,' he said. 'Things are beginning to move and I must ride again soon. I'd like a fresh horse and if you have something to eat I'd be mighty grateful.'

'Of course, Johnny, come along inside,' said Kathy.

Clint Arthurs came hurrying up. 'I'll see to your horse, Johnny,' he offered.

'Saddle me another,' said Johnny. 'I'll ride again in half an hour. Things are beginning to move. I know for sure that Nick didn't commit suicide.'

Kathy gasped. There was a look of grateful thanks in her eyes which began to fill with tears.

'Ken Petch saw what happened. I'll tell you all about it inside.' Johnny looked at Clint who was about to lead the horse away. 'Stay close to the house,' he instructed. 'I don't know how things will turn out but look after Mrs Sheridan.'

'You can depend on us,' reassured Clint. As he headed for the stable Johnny followed Kathy into the house.

After a wash and change of clothes Johnny

felt much fresher and, as he enjoyed a meal of steak, he told Kathy about the recent events. Johnny was anxious to be on his way to the Twisted F where he had a feeling that the solution to the mystery lay; but before leaving the Three Rs he studied Nick's maps again paying more attention to the lie of the Three Rs and the Twisted F in relation to those ranches which had already sold out. He saw that if one person got the lot they would own all the valley, together with all the land at both ends where it spilled out on the vast stretches of range. The one strip they had not known about was that which Dan Neale hoped to purchase.

Johnny had much to occupy his mind as he rode steadily northwards through the hills towards the Twisted F. As he topped the last rise which dropped into the valley leading to the ranch he pulled his horse to a sudden halt and turned it quickly below the skyline. He dropped from the saddle and crawled quickly to the top of the slope to peer cautiously into the valley. Two horsemen were riding at a fast pace in the direction of the ranch. One was a big man on a big horse whilst his slimmer companion rode easily, one arm hanging loosely by his side.

'Simpson and Webster!' muttered Johnny

to himself. His eyes shone with excitement. Was he right? Did the Twisted F hold the key to the recent happenings around Newlin?

Johnny slipped quickly to his horse and, hanging back some distance behind the two men, shadowed them carefully from the ridge. When the ranch came into sight Johnny pulled to a halt and watched the two men ride in. He was anxious to get to the house, hoping to find out if the saloon owner and the sheriff were meeting the seldom seen Amos North, but he knew that now he must exercise the utmost caution. He studied the layout of the ranch carefully. The main building was a long low ranch-house set some distance away from the other buildings, which were situated on the far side of the house from Johnny. Beyond the bunkhouse and the stables were several corrals in one of which he could see three men breaking-in some horses.

Durango worked his way along the ridge until he judged he was behind the house. He slipped from the saddle and, when he crept to the top of the slope, he found he was looking down on the back of the house. The men were still working with horses and if he was careful in his approach he reckoned he could reach the house without being seen.

He slid over the edge of the ridge quickly keeping as low as possible so as to break the skyline for the least possible moment. He edged his way quickly downwards, using a slight hollow in the slope as cover keeping his eyes on the windows at the back of the house, hoping no one looked out. He saw no movement and reckoned he had reached the veranda, which completely surrounded the house, without being seen. Striding over the low rail he flattened himself against the wall and inched his way forward to the nearest window, beside the back door. He peered in cautiously but his attention was so concentrated that he was unaware of the door opening quietly behind him. A cowboy with Colt drawn stepped out and with one swift blow brought the barrel of the gun crashing down on the back of Johnny's head. His brain seemed to explode and darkness swept in upon him as he pitched to the boards and lay still.

# EIGHT

When Curt Simpson and Mart Webster pulled to a halt outside the Twisted F ranch-house Floyd Readman, the foreman, stepped out to meet them.

'Has Mister North arrived yet?' asked Simpson. There was a worried look on his face as he swung from the saddle and stepped on to the veranda.

The foreman nodded. 'Hasn't been here many minutes, he's just changing. Come inside.'

The broad-shouldered, powerfully built, muscular foreman led the way into a room which was elegantly furnished. A large mahogany desk stood at one end and one wall was lined with bookshelves. It bore the marks of an educated man with very personal tastes and Curt Simpson was a little envious of Amos North and his background as they waited for him to make his appearance.

Five minutes passed before the door opened and North stepped into the room. He was of medium height and medium build but held himself very erect seeming to add to his height. His long thin face was brown, belying the paleness beneath. The brown hair had a natural tendency to wave and the slight greying at the temples seemed to add a distinguished look to his fifty years. His deep brown eyes were penetrative and missed nothing but exuded no warmth what-so-ever. Here was a man used to giving orders and used to being obeyed. Authority seemed to generate from him in such a way that men, more physically capable than he, dare not question him.

'Hello, Simpson, Webster,' he greeted with a faint smile. 'I did not expect to see you both so soon after my arrival.' He paused for a moment looking hard at Simpson. 'Something is troubling you,' he said. 'All is not going well, hasn't Mrs Sheridan and Neale decided to sell yet?'

'No,' replied Simpson. 'The trouble is that Farrow slipped up and let Durango out-smart him.'

'What!' North gasped. 'I thought everything was fixed up before I left.' There was a measure of annoyance in his voice.

'So it was,' agreed Simpson, 'but this Durango's a smart hombre. In spite of all efforts he's still around.' The saloon owner went on to tell North of the happenings since Johnny Durango arrived in Newlin.

North listened carefully, pulling hard at a cheroot which he lit when Simpson started his explanations.

'This man has got to be dealt with and dealt with quickly,' he pointed out at the conclusion of Simpson's story. 'He's getting too nosey and if we want to keep things our way he's got to be taken care of, but I can understand Webster's point in playing it carefully after Sheridan's murder.'

'He might be walking right into our hands,' said Webster and went on to tell North how he had followed Durango and what he had overheard at the Circle A.

North smiled when he had finished. 'This is just what we want,' he said. 'Durango's going to ride right into a neat little trap and find himself on a murder charge. Webster, you'll see that it sticks and we'll be rid of both Durango and Neale.' He turned to his foreman. 'Station yourself just inside the back door. I figure this Durango will be anxious to know what's going on here. He may ride in openly paying a social call to look both myself and the place over. If he does then we can easily deal with him. On the other hand he may try to take a look round without us knowing, in that case Floyd can take him.'

The foreman nodded and left to take up a position near the back door. Five minutes passed and then Readman tensed himself when he heard the faint creak of a board on the veranda. A moment later he eased the door slightly open and, seeing the figure of a cowboy move towards the window which he knew to be open, he slipped his Colt from his holster. Gently he opened the door until it was wide enough for him to slip out, then suddenly he moved with the speed of a snake and before the cowboy knew where he was and what was happening, Readman brought his Colt crashing down on the man's head. As the man pitched to the boards a smile of satisfaction split the foreman's face. He holstered his Colt and, grasping the unconscious man's shirt in his huge fists, dragged him inside to drop him unceremoniously in front of the three men.

'That him?' asked North.

Simpson nodded. 'Sure is,' he grinned. North's face was serious as he looked at the three men in front of him. 'Curt, you get back to town; Floyd, take three of the boys and bushwack Neale, there is only one trail he'll take from his spread to Jenkins' place. If Durango comes round a slight tap will put him under again. Mart you had better not ride with them in case they are seen by anyone; stay here a while then follow them.' They discussed the plan in more detail and soon Curt Simpson was heading for Newlin and Floyd Readman with three of the Twisted F cowboys rode briskly away leading a horse across the back of which drooped the unconscious figure of Johnny Durango.

When they reached the trail which they expected Dan Neale to take Floyd Readman quickly found a group of boulders above a slight hollow through which the trail passed.

'This should do fine,' he said pulling his rifle from its scabbard. 'I reckon he'll be an easy target from here.' He instructed his two cowboys to scout the trail in both directions to make sure Dan Neale had not passed through the hollow. If he had then the man who headed in the direction of Jenkins' spread was told to deal with him but the other man was instructed to warn Readman of Neale's approach if he saw him.

When the two rode off Readman settled down to wait after making sure that Johnny Durango would not regain consciousness for some time. Twenty minutes passed before Floyd heard the sound of approaching hoofs and saw one of the men returning.

'I got within sight of Jenkins' house and have not seen him,' the man reported.

'Good, then it looks as if he hasn't passed through here yet,' commented Readman.

A few minutes later his observation was confirmed when the second man returned to report that Dan Neale was on his way. Readman smiled coldly and settled himself more comfortably between two boulders. A short while later they saw Dan Neale start to ride into the hollow. An excitement seized Readman as he raised his rifle to his shoulder. He waited a few moments until Dan came nearer and then, as he lined his sights on the brown shirt of the rider, an intense calmness descended on him. His hands were steady; his brain was cool and with meticulous care he followed the rider with his rifle then slowly he moved it slightly ahead of the moving target. Satisfied that his estimation was correct Readman gently squeezed the trigger. The roar reverberated from the boulders and rocked across the hollow. Dan Neale stiffened as if struck by a giant hand then fell sideways and as his horse, frightened by the noise, set off into a gallop he was pitched from the saddle to lie face downwards on the ground.

'Check him,' ordered Readman and one of the men drew his Colt and rode towards Dan Neale.

Readman watched for a moment and then pushed himself to his feet. He moved swiftly to Johnny Durango and drew the unconscious man's Colt from its holster. Pointing the gun across the grassland he fired once before returning the Colt to the holster. He turned his attention to the man riding towards Dan Neale and saw the man pull to a halt, climb from his horse and examine the body. When the man waved Floyd knew his aim had been true. He grinned as he turned to the man beside him.

'C'm on,' he said.

They swung into their saddles and, leading the third horse, galloped down into the hollow. When they pulled to a halt they unfastened the still unconscious Durango, laid him on the ground and sent his horse stamping a short distance away. Readman drew Durango's Colt and put it into the unconscious man's hand. He looked around, and, satisfied that all was as he meant it to be, he nodded to his two companions and all three set their horses up the slope.

When they topped the rise they saw a lone horseman riding slowly in their direction.

Readman grinned and set his horse towards the rider.

'He's all yours,' called Readman as he pulled his horse to a halt alongside Mart Webster. 'It was as easy as falling off a horse wasn't it boys?'

His two companions laughed raucously and put their horses into a fast gallop across the grassland in the direction of the Twisted F.

'You're in good time,' grinned Readman. 'Durango won't come round for a while.'

Webster said nothing and with a cursory nod put his horse back into a walking pace towards the hollow. Readman with a yell kicked his horse into a fast gallop in pursuit of the two men who were racing across the grassland.

The Sheriff of Newlin halted at the top of the rise, surveyed the scene below him and decided to wait where he was. From this position he had a good view of the country-side, and should anyone by chance approach the hollow he would be able to head them off before they were witnesses to the grim scene. Nothing stirred on the landscape and Webster began to get impatient for action. Would Durango never regain consciousness? Had Readman dealt too severely with him?

Twenty minutes passed and Webster was about to ride into the hollow to examine the silent forms when he noticed a slight stirring. Mart tensed himself, eased his gun out of the holster and narrowed his eyes as he watched the two figures below him.

Johnny Durango became aware of a mad pounding in his head. His brain spun, everything seemed to be in a whirl. Slowly his mind cleared; it seemed an eternity before his last recollection focused in his mind. The Twisted F! What had happened? Where was he? His eyes flickered open and he was aware of the blue canopy above him still filled with the glare of a lowering sun. He moved his head but it pained him, then he realized he held something hard in his hand. He lifted it up and stared stupidly at his Colt. Why was it there? Where was he? Johnny struggled to sit up. He glanced around and his gaze settled on the silent figure lying face downwards on the earth. He looked at his gun then back at the man, and a cold feeling of horror gripped at his heart. He pushed himself to his feet unsteadily and staggered as he stepped slowly towards the body. Bending forward he turned the head so that he could discover the identity of the man. Johnny straightened with horror, the shock seemed to make him recoil and cleared his brain.

'Dan Neale!' The words escaped from his lips in a long drawn out whisper.

He stared unbelievingly at the body, oblivious to the sound of a galloping horse until it was almost upon him, Johnny spun round to find the Sheriff of Newlin covering him with a Colt and pulling hard on the reins to bring his horse to a dust stirring halt.

'Drop that gun, Durango,' shouted the sheriff.

Johnny his mind in a whirl hesitated. The sheriff's Colt roared and the bullet whined unpleasantly close to Johnny's head.

'I might not be so easy with the next one!' called the lawman.

Johnny slackened his grip on his Colt and the gun dropped at his feet.

'Kick it away!' ordered Webster.

Johnny did as he was told. His thoughts raced. He knew how things must look to the sheriff.

'I didn't do this,' protested Johnny. 'The last thing I remember was being at the Twisted F. I reckon someone planted me here after killin' Dan Neale to try to pin the murder on me.'

Webster sneered contemptuously. 'You

can always think of some excuse, Durango. I come on you standing over Neale's body, a gun in your hand. I'm arresting you fer the murder of Dan Neale.'

'Have a look at my gun,' shouted Johnny. 'It hasn't been fired.'

The sheriff swung from the saddle, moved cautiously forward and, keeping an eye on Johnny, picked up the Colt. He examined it quickly then looked hard at Johnny.

'One bullet fired,' he hissed.

Johnny was startled. Whoever wanted him out of the way was thorough and it looked as if Amos North was involved in the whole affair. In fact Johnny now felt pretty sure he must be the brains behind it all. But how had he known Dan Neale would be riding that way? Why did he want all his land?

'Git on your horse,' snapped Webster interrupting Johnny's racing thoughts. 'An' don't try anythin',' he warned. 'I'll hev no hesitation in droppin' you.'

Johnny knew it was useless to argue and soon the two men were riding to Newlin at a steady pace.

Darkness had settled on Newlin when the two men rode along the main street. There were a number of cowboys on the sidewalk and word soon got round that the sheriff was bringing Durango in at the point of a gun. A sizeable crowd had gathered near the sheriff's office and speculation ran wild as to what had happened. The sheriff bustled Durango inside and soon had him locked behind bars. Curt Simpson had kept a look out for the sheriff and when he saw him ride in with Durango he knew all had gone according to plan. Now he had to play his part. It was not long before the people of Newlin knew that the sheriff had caught Durango, with a gun in his hand, standing over the body of Dan Neale.

During the evening Simpson kept the story circulating in the Gay Lady, praising the qualities of Dan Neale and branding Johnny Durango as a cold-blooded killer who murdered without apparent motive. As more drink was consumed so the feeling ran higher.

It was about ten o'clock when a horse pounded along the main street and drew to a halt outside the sheriff's office. Wes Jenkins swung out of the saddle and strode into the sheriff's office were Mart Webster was seated behind the desk cleaning his gun.

'Is it right that Dan Neale was shot this evening on the trail to my place?' asked Wes coming straight to the point.

'Sure is,' replied Mart. 'I caught the killer standing over him.'

'Who was it?' queried Wes.

'Hombre by the name of Durango,' answered Mart. 'Stranger to these parts but had been on friendly terms with Dan since he rode in. Why are you interested in it?'

'Dan was ridin' to my place by arrangement,' said Wes. 'He was goin' to buy a piece of land off me.'

'Land?' The sheriff appeared puzzled.

'Yes, a strip I own between Dan's spread and the Twisted F. Not many people know that land belongs to me. With all this land buyin' goin' on Dan was interested in havin' it an' I wanted to sell, but as a matter of fact only he and I knew of the deal.'

The sheriff stroked his chin thoughtfully. 'Then it looks as if Dan confided in Durango, then he bushwhacked him to stop him reachin' you.'

Jenkins started at Webster. 'You mean this Durango wanted the land?'

Webster grinned to himself. The seed of suspicion had been sown and Jenkins had taken it. 'Sure why not?'

'Then he could be behind all this other land buyin' which has caused so much trouble,' mused Jenkins.

143

Webster agreed. He knew Jenkins liked a drink and would no doubt pay the Gay Lady a visit. If Curt Simpson had played the game correctly feeling against Durango would be running high in the Gay Lady and Wes Jenkins' visit would add more to the tension. Soon Durango would be out of the way for good and he, the sheriff, exonerated from all blame after doing his best to stop the mob. Mart's thoughts, which were racing far ahead, were suddenly interrupted by Jenkins.

'You've now got a motive,' he pointed out, 'but you'd better ask the prisoner if he knew where Neale was goin', that will confirm it.'

Webster agreed and, pushing himself from his chair, entered the cell block. Johnny looked up from the hard boards which served as a bunk when he heard the sheriff walk in.

'Durango, do you know where Dan Neale was goin'?' asked Webster suddenly.

'Sure,' replied Johnny. 'He told me earlier he was goin' to see Wes Jenkins about the purchase of some land.'

Jenkins who had come to stand in the doorway to the cell block stiffened. 'There you are, sheriff, the motive,' he called. 'Only Dan and I knew about our deal.'

Johnny gasped when he realized how he

had been tricked into supplying a motive for murder.

Webster grinned evilly through the bars. 'Thanks Durango,' he said. 'I knew you'd come to a sticky end.'

Johnny's lips tightened; his eyes smouldered with hate. 'I guess you did,' he hissed, 'seeing that you are in on the frame-up.'

Webster laughed loudly and turned to Jenkins. 'Wes,' he grinned, 'this hombre reckons he was at the Twisted F and remembers nothing after that.'

'Soon see if that's true,' said Wes. 'I saw Floyd Readman, the Twisted F foreman, goin' into the Gay Lady. Why not get him over here?'

'Good idea,' smiled Webster. He called to his deputy and instructed him to bring Floyd Readman from the saloon.

When the two men returned a little over five minutes later Webster took Readman to Durango's cell.

'Have you seen this man before, Floyd?' he asked.

Readman shook his head. 'No,' he replied a puzzled look on his face. 'What's this all about?'

'Durango reckons he was at the Twisted F,' explained the sheriff. 'Says that's the last thing he can remember. Figures he was knocked out there and dumped by Dan Neale's body.'

'Wal I was around the Twisted F until I rode into town a couple of hours ago. I never saw him,' replied Readman.

'Thanks,' said the sheriff and the two men walked from the cell block leaving Johnny protesting his innocence.

Wes Jenkins and Floyd Readman bade the sheriff good-bye and crossed the street together to the Gay Lady. All the talk in the saloon was on the killing and Curt Simpson was helping to build up the tempers of the men by adding a word here and there. Everyone knew that Floyd Readman had been called from the saloon in connection with the affair and they eagerly awaited his return for the latest developments. When he re-entered the saloon there was a lull in the conversations and everyone looked towards the Twisted F foreman as he crossed to the bar with Wes Jenkins.

Curt Simpson seized his opportunity. 'When are they goin' to hang him, Floyd?' he shouted.

'Guess when he's had a trial,' replied Readman smiling to himself. 'He's tryin' to use the Twisted F as an alibi. Says he was out there an' that we laid him cold and left him by the body.'

Curt laughed loudly. 'That's some story,' he yelled. 'How did he expect anyone to swallow that one?'

There was a roar of laughter from the occupants of the saloon.

'What's he reckon your motives were?' called Curt.

'Search me,' replied Floyd.

'Twisted F had no motives,' shouted Jenkins, 'but Durango had.' There was a gasp from the crowd and a silence settled on the room. 'Dan was comin' to buy some land from me,' went on Jenkins, 'no one else knew about it as far as I knew but Durango admits Dan told him about it earlier today.'

Curt grinned to himself. Innocently Wes Jenkins, his temper roused at the killing, was playing right into his hands. Curt Simpson was not slow to seize the opportunity.

'Looks as though Dan Neale was killed fer a piece of land,' he shouted. 'Durango wanted to stop him and no doubt would have made an offer for it to Wes when this had all died down.'

There was a murmur of agreement round the saloon. Shock at the reason for the cold-blooded killing turned to hate against the man in the jail.

'Dan Neale was a good citizen,' shouted someone.

'Reckon we shouldn't wait for the circuit judge!' yelled another.

There was a roar from the crowd and Curt Simpson fanned the flame. He saw that before long the temper of the crowd would boil over and then a word at the right moment would easily turn them into a lynch-mob.

# NINE

Johnny Durango lay on his back staring at the ceiling of his cell unaware of the feeling that was running high against him in the Gay Lady. His mind was turning over the events and facts as he knew them.

He was certain now that Amos North was involved in the whole affair, possibly was even the brains behind everything but Johnny could not find a reason for the buying of the land in the neighbourhood. Maybe the answer lay away from Newlin; maybe if enquiries could be made in the east where North owned land he would find an answer. If only he could get out of jail! He grew impatient and annoyed with himself but he realized how cleverly he had been framed with no chance of proving his innocence. As his mind drifted back to the Twisted F he had a feeling that he had been expected. He had seen Simpson and Webster arrive at the Twisted F and this, to his mind, tied them with North but they could not have known of his intentions. Only Dan knew about

149

those and Dan would... Suddenly Johnny stiffened with excitement as he realized the answer.

Whoever knew about his intended visit to the Twisted F must have overheard him tell Dan and if they'd heard that then they must have also heard that Dan was going to see Wes Jenkins about the land. Dan realized he must have been followed from Newlin when he had left Vernon Petch's. Mart Webster had left Petch's only a few minutes before and must have waited to follow him but, having overheard his conversation with Dan, Webster must have contacted Simpson and then the pair had ridden to consult the boss. From there on North had planned the whole thing; Neale stopped from putting through the land deal and the murder used to frame Johnny and get him out of the way.

Johnny jumped to his feet. Somehow he must get out. He paced the floor impatiently, racking his brain to find a means of escape.

Three minutes passed but they seemed like an eternity to Johnny as his mind pounded in its search for freedom.

'Johnny!' The voice was so low that Durango thought his ears were deceiving him. 'Johnny!' The urgency in the tone carried to the prisoner and, when he realized it came from outside, his heart began to pound with hope.

He stepped quickly on to his bunk and, grasping the iron bars across the window, eased himself upwards on to his toes until he could peer out. He saw a shadowy form standing in the alley but because of the darkness he could not make out who it was.

'Who is it?' he whispered.

'Vernon Petch,' came the reply. There was a note of relief in the voice at hearing him and having found Johnny. 'There's trouble being stirred up in the Gay Lady,' went on Petch quickly. 'Curt Simpson seems to be pushing it hard; won't be long before that mob is marchin' down here.'

Johnny stiffened at the news. So that was how they planned to get rid of him! No doubt Mart Webster would put up a token resistance so that he could not be blamed for the lynching.

'I've brought you a gun,' continued Petch, 'figured you deserve some sort of a chance.' He thrust a Colt upwards to Johnny who took it with a thankful, urgent, eagerness.

'Thanks, Vernon,' replied Johnny. 'I'm near gettin' to the bottom of this whole affair but I've got to get out of here. Will you step in a bit deeper?'

151

'You saved my son, Johnny; what do you want me to do?' A feeling of relief flooded over Johnny when he heard Petch's reply.

'Get the sheriff through to me on some pretext or other,' he said.

Vernon Petch hurried along the dark alley to the main street and Johnny, hiding the Colt inside his shirt, lay down on his bunk.

When Petch reached the corner of the building he was startled by the loudness of the noise coming from the Gay Lady. He realized that Curt Simpson had done his work well and any moment now an angry mob, all reason gone, would pour from the saloon and march to the jail. There was not a moment to lose. Petch hurried to the office door and stepped quickly inside. The sheriff looked up, startled by the suddenness of the entry.

'Sheriff, there's a mob gathering in the Gay Lady, figuring on lynchin' Durango,' said Petch an urgent uneasiness in his voice.

'They won't get near him,' replied Webster. 'I can handle them with my deputy's help.'

'I guess you can,' said Petch, 'but I figure on stoppin' them altogether. I have some information proving Durango's innocence.'

Webster was startled by this statement but

he hid his feelings. 'All right,' he said, 'you'd better let me hear it quick.'

'I want Durango to hear it at the same time,' answered Petch.

The sheriff looked annoyed but he realized he had to go along with Petch in order to appear above suspicion and keep his standing as lawman. As he stood up he took the cell keys from the desk.

'Guess if that mob gets too handy these will be better in my pocket,' he grinned. When the time came both Petch and his deputy would be witnesses that he had had the keys on his person.

The two men had reached the door to the cell block when the deputy who was watching the main street from the window cried out.

'They're comin', Mart!' There was a touch of alarm in his voice.

The sheriff spun round. 'Lock that door,' he ordered, 'an' get out the rifles.' He looked at Petch. 'C'm on,' he said, 'better make it snappy.'

As the deputy hurried to do as he was ordered the sheriff, followed by Petch, walked quickly to Johnny's cell. Johnny pushed himself to his feet, alarm showing on his face.

'What's that?' he asked.

'Guess the townsfolk are riled up at you,' answered Webster.

'Lynch mob!' gasped Johnny. He moved forward to the bars of the cell. He shot a glance at Petch. 'What's he doin' here?'

'Reckons he has proof that you didn't kill Neale,' replied the sheriff. 'Don't see how that can be when I saw you with a gun, standing over Neale.' He turned to Petch. 'Out with it, what's your story?'

In the instance that he turned Johnny drew his Colt.

'Jest this, Webster,' he rapped.

Startled by the sudden change in the tone of Durango's voice the sheriff spun round but recoiled when he saw the cold muzzle of a Colt aimed at him from Durango's hand.

'What the...' he started.

He was interrupted as Petch jerked the Colt from the sheriff's holster.

'The keys, quick,' hissed Petch.

The lawman hesitated but the presence of a gun in his back made his mind up for him. Reluctantly he fumbled for the keys and, when he produced them, Petch grabbed them and quickly unlocked the cell door. Johnny stepped outside and motioned Webster into the cell. As the lawman passed him

Johnny whipped the barrel of the Colt across his head. He pitched to the floor without a sound.

The roar of the mob had been gradually growing louder. It was an ugly sound which sent a shiver through Johnny. He was glad he was on the right side of the bars. He indicated the back door to Petch who hurried to find the right key whilst Johnny watched the door into the sheriff's office.

'Mart, hurry up! They're in a wild mood,' shouted the deputy, fear and concern in his voice.

Johnny glanced anxiously at Petch and in that moment Vernon found the right key. He swung the door open and the two men hurried down the back street with the crescendo of the howling mob rising from the other side of the building.

The deputy watched anxiously at the window. He felt an awful tightening of his chest as the mob seemed to fill and flow along the street towards the sheriff's office. The front row of men walked with a steady but determined step and in the centre one huge bulk of a man seemed to loom above the others – Curt Simpson. Behind, the mass seemed to heave and dip in uneven step. Light from the buildings spilled across the mob and one or two men carried flaming torches which added a flickering grimness to the scene.

The deputy had never seen a lynch mob before but he had heard about them, about their ugliness, viciousness and unreasonableness. It needed a strong determined man to face and deal with a lynch mob in an ugly mood. He wished the sheriff would hurry. He realized his hands were wet and clammy where he gripped his rifle. Brushing his forehead with his left hand he found beads of sweat in spite of the chillness which gripped him. The mob was getting too near for his liking; the sheriff ought to be here; what was happening in the cells? Petch was taking his time telling his story.

'Mart!' he yelled over his shoulder. There was a touch of fear in his voice.

He shifted uneasily on his feet. There was no reply. Suddenly he swung round and strode to the cell block. He gasped when he saw the open door of the cell and the crumpled form of the sheriff. His thoughts tumbled as he jumped to the sheriff's side and dropped beside him on one knee. He turned the lawman over and Webster, a groan escaping from his lips, struggled to sit up. The deputy helped him and supported him against one knee.

Webster's head spun. The whole place seemed to be a whirl of bars. He forced his eyes open and the spinning seemed to stop with a sudden jerk but his head throbbed as if a herd of horses were galloping through it. He raised a hand and felt his head gingerly. From somewhere a voice seemed to be speaking.

'What happened?' asked the deputy.

Mart turned his head towards the sound and when he saw his deputy kneeling beside him the full realization of what had happened hit him.

'Petch pulled a fast one,' he muttered struggling to get to his feet.

The deputy helped him and supported him as he walked into his office. The roar outside was louder. The deputy glanced anxiously at Mart.

'What are we goin' to do about them?' he asked.

The sheriff took a gun from the drawer of his desk and slipped it into his holster. 'Tell them what's happened,' he muttered grimly, 'that'll disperse them quicker than anything.' He walked unsteadily to the door and followed by his deputy stepped outside.

The mob had almost reached the office

157

and when the two officials appeared a great roar greeted them. Curt Simpson stepped forward.

'We want that no-good...' he yelled but his voice faded as the sheriff stepped forward and held up his hand. Curt saw the white, drawn face of the lawman and he knew that something had gone wrong.

The sheriff stood in the same attitude for a few moments waiting for the noise to subside. There was something in Webster's manner which caused the mob to feel uneasy and the trailing away of Simpson's voice added to that feeling.

'Quiet!' shouted Mart. He paused then came straight to the point. 'Durango's escaped!' A murmur ran through the crowd. It was gaining volume when Mart yelled louder.

'Hold it! I'm goin' after Durango now. It will help me if you will all get about your own business.' Mart began to exert his authority as a lawman. 'If you're all running around lookin' for Durango it will only lead to confusion and maybe more killing. Four of us can deal with the situation better than a lot. I'll take my deputy, Simpson and...' he hesitated momentarily glancing at the faces in front of him '...and you Readman.'

Webster spun on his heel and strode into the office as if the matter was settled. When he reappeared a few moments later with his Stetson the crowd was already breaking up into small groups and dispersing along the street.

'What happened?' asked Simpson. Webster detected a note of annoyance in his voice.

'Vernon Petch pulled a fast one,' replied Webster. 'I reckon that's where they'll head for first.'

The four men with sheriff in the lead hurried along the sidewalk towards the edge of town.

'You're in this deep, Vernon,' called Johnny as the two men raced along the back street.

'I know,' replied Petch. 'Reckon I'd better leave town with you. There are two horses in my stable.'

'Good,' said Johnny.

The two men left any further talking until later and proceeded quickly but cautiously through the darkened back streets. Once they reached the town they hurried to Vernon's house. They approached the building carefully wondering whether the deputy had been smart enough to guess their intentions.

They satisfied themselves quickly that no one was about.

'We won't have long but I must see Emily,' said Petch after they had made sure no one was about.

'Right,' replied Johnny. 'I'll be saddling the horses.'

The two men hurried their respective ways and Johnny had almost finished his task when Petch ran into the stables a few minutes later.

'Emily's worried,' he panted, 'but she and Ken will be all right. Webster daren't harm them.'

When the horses were ready the two men swung into the saddles and rode from the stable.

'We'll head for the Three Rs,' called Johnny.

Petch nodded and they kicked their mounts forward breaking into a fast gallop away from Newlin.

When the sheriff came in sight of Petch's house he halted.

'Deputy, you an' Floyd cover the back,' he ordered. 'Simpson you watch the front door and keep me covered.'

When he was satisfied that the three men

were in position Mart Webster, with Colt drawn moved cautiously forward to the house. His eyes moved everywhere trying to pierce the darkness around him as he searched for the two men. He saw nothing and when he reached the house he flattened himself against the wall and inched his way towards the window from which a light shone through drawn curtains. Through a gap in the curtains he saw Mrs Petch laying the table for a meal and her son reading a book. He could see little more of the room but he reckoned Mrs Petch and Ken were the only occupants.

Webster moved quickly to the front door, slipped his gun back into its holster, and rapped loudly on the woodwork. A few moments later the door opened to reveal Mrs Petch.

'Evenin' ma'am,' Webster touched his sombrero politely. 'Is your husband in?'

'I'm afraid he isn't,' replied Mrs Petch.

'Has he been in during the last ten minutes?' asked the sheriff.

'Is anything wrong?' asked Mrs Petch trying to waste time.

'Your husband helped Durango escape from jail,' said the sheriff. 'I figured he'd made for here, have you seen him?'

Mrs Petch had no need to answer the question for at that moment a shout came from the direction of the stable.

'The horses have gone!' It was the deputy and he came running towards the sheriff. 'We got into position at the back of the house then I reckoned it would be an idea to check the stables,' he explained. 'I left Floyd, worked my way slowly into the stable in case Durango and Petch were about. There was no one but the horses have gone.'

'C'm on,' cried the sheriff ignoring Mrs Petch's protestations. 'Floyd! Curt!' he yelled.

The two men ran after the two lawmen who were already running towards their horses.

'They've been there,' called out Mart. 'Taken the horses. Let's check the Three Rs.'

The four men raced to their horses and a few minutes later were thundering out of Newlin at an earth-pounding gallop.

Johnny Durango cast many an anxious glance at Vernon Petch as their horses stretched themselves in gallop along the trail away from Newlin. He knew that Petch was not a horseman but admired the way he stuck grimly beside him. They swung off the trail onto the dirt track which crossed the hill to the Three Rs. The ground became rougher and Johnny had to ease the pace but as yet there was no sign of pursuit. He was glad when the bulk of the buildings showed up black in the darkness. He had already formulated his plan of action and figuring that Webster would check all likely places to get his hands on him knew he had not long to linger at the Three Rs.

The sound of galloping animals brought Kathy Sheridan on to the veranda with the three hired hands. They kept to the shadows, guns at the ready but when the two horsemen pulled to a sliding halt close to the house and they recognized them they hurried forward.

'What's wrong?' asked Kathy reading trouble in the swiftness of the approach.

'Things went wrong out at the Twisted F; landed myself in jail,' explained Johnny as the two men stepped on to the veranda. 'Vernon broke me out. He'll tell you all about it after I've gone.'

There was a look of alarm on Kathy's face. 'Don't ride anymore, Johnny,' she pleaded.

'Got to,' replied Johnny. 'I guess it won't be long before Mart Webster decides to check here. Keep Vernon hidden; I'll take his horse and turn it loose somewhere on the way; that might help to throw the sheriff off the trail.'

Kathy started to protest but Johnny cut her short.

'I think I'll soon get to the bottom of this whole thing,' he said. 'I'm goin' to do some checking up on Amos North; I figure the answer lies in his past. I'd like some food with me please, Kathy.'

Kathy Sheridan knew it was useless to try to keep Johnny back. She realized she would be helping him if she did as he asked.

'Sure, Johnny,' she replied. 'We'll see Vernon is all right.'

She hurried into the house and whilst she packed some food for him Durango enjoyed a cup of coffee.

'Be careful, Johnny,' she said as he swung into the saddle.

'I'll be all right,' he answered. 'Don't worry. He spurred his horse and, leading Petch's mount, galloped away into the darkness.

# TEN

When the hoofbeats faded into the distance Kathy hurried into the house. She looked anxiously at Vernon Petch.

'What happened?' she asked.

Vernon told his story quickly. 'I'll be an embarrassment to you here, Mrs Sheridan,' he concluded. 'If I slip away now...'

'Nonsense,' cut in Kathy. 'I'm grateful for what you've done. Somebody planned the whole thing very carefully and hoped to get Johnny out of the way for good. It's a good job you were around but we must keep you out of the sheriff's hands until Johnny gets back.' She turned to her three hired cowboys who had listened grimly to Petch's account of the recent incidents. 'We'll soon be having a visit from the sheriff. Wes, keep watch from the veranda, Clint and Bud you go to the bunkhouse; act as if nothing had happened. When you hear them coming Wes, warn us and then go to the bunkhouse. From then on act natural.'

The three men nodded and hurried from

the house.

'I'm mighty grateful,' started Vernon.

'Save your thanks,' interrupted Kathy. 'When the sheriff arrives hide in my bedroom; there's a big cupboard in there but I think I can prevent him from searching my room.'

The next twenty minutes seemed an age as they waited and Kathy was beginning to think that their supposition was wrong when there was a warning tap on the door.

'Quick into the bedroom,' said Kathy springing to her feet.

Vernon Petch hurried into the bedroom and Kathy closed the door behind him. She waited until the sound of horses drew near to the house and then, with rifle in her hand, stepped out on to the veranda. Four horsemen were pulling to a halt.

'Stay in your saddles,' she called from the shadows. 'There's a rifle pointing right at you.'

'Hold it, Mrs Sheridan,' shouted Webster. 'It's the sheriff. I'd like a word with you.'

Kathy moved forward. 'I'm sorry,' she said. 'Couldn't see who it was in the darkness and it pays to be careful. Come along inside.'

The four men were swinging from the saddles when the door of the bunkhouse swung open and the three hired men ran out.

'You all right, Mrs Sheridan,' called Wes.

'Yes thanks,' answered Kathy. She was glad they had done the natural thing and appeared at the sound of horses. 'It's only the sheriff.'

The three men turned to retrace their steps to the bunkhouse.

'I think you had all better hear what I have to say,' called the sheriff. 'Mind if we all come inside Mrs Sheridan?'

'Not at all,' answered Kathy.

She led the way into the house and turned to face the sheriff.

'Is anything wrong?' she asked calmly. 'You're not often this way at this time of night.'

'When did you last see Johnny Durango?' asked Mart Webster ignoring Kathy's question.

'During the late afternoon,' answered Kathy. 'Said he was going to the Twisted F.'

'He hasn't been here since?' queried the lawman.

'No,' answered Kathy. Concern showed on her face. 'Has something happened to him?'

'He killed Dan Neale and then Vernon Petch broke him out of jail.'

'What!' gasped Kathy disbelievingly.

The three hired hands looked equally surprised.

''Fraid so ma'm,' went on Webster. 'We figured they might have ridden this way seein' as how Durango had been staying with you. Mind if we take a look round?'

'Really, sheriff, don't you take my word?' said Kathy pretending to be hurt by the sheriff's disbelief.

'I'm sorry,' answered Webster, 'but as a lawman I must take every precaution, besides they may be hangin' about without you knowing.' He turned to his deputy. 'Take Curt and Floyd and take a look around out side, bunkhouse, stables, the lot.'

When the three men had left the house, Webster glanced at Kathy.

'I'm afraid I'll have to search the house,' he said.

'Help yourself,' replied Kathy annoyance showing on her face. 'But you won't find anyone.'

Kathy and her three men waited impatiently listening to Mart Webster moving through the house. He returned to the hall and made towards the door of Kathy's bedroom.

'You don't think I've got them in my bedroom, do you, sheriff?' There was a note of indignation in Kathy's voice.

The sheriff hesitated. He glanced at the door and turned. He shrugged his shoulders.

'I guess not,' he said and walked to the outside door where he stood waiting impatiently for the return of the men who had ridden with him.

Kathy hid the sense of relief which flooded over her and she hoped it would not be long before the sheriff left. Her desire was soon granted when, a few moments later, the three men returned.

'No sign of anyone,' reported the deputy. 'We've checked everywhere. There are no recently ridden horses in the stable.'

Annoyance darkened the sheriff's face. He had felt sure that Durango would head for the Three Rs. Amos North was not going to like this and he would get the blame. He knew North could not stand inefficiency and dealt ruthlessly with anyone who slipped up on his plans. His mind was in a turmoil wondering what to do next. He must get Durango. Suddenly as if he had made a decision he turned.

'Good night, Mrs Sheridan, I'm sorry we

bothered you,' he said quietly.

He strode from the house followed by the three men. They swung into the saddles and headed away from the ranch in the direction of Newlin at a steady trot.

Once they had cleared the hill behind the house Mart Webster called a halt.

'Deputy,' he said. 'Ride back to town and be on hand there in case anything develops; I'm goin' to do some more searching.'

The man nodded and put his horse into a trot. When the deputy had disappeared into the darkness Mart turned to Simpson.

'I don't like it Curt,' he said. 'North is goin' to have to know an' he won't be pleased about it.'

'I'll say he won't,' agreed Simpson. 'Durango must be caught. Things were goin' fine until Petch butted in.'

'I'll say. I have a feeling Durango's been out here,' went on Webster. 'I'm goin' to scout round, see if I can pick up his trail. Curt, I reckon you an' Floyd had better head for the Twisted F; tell North what's happened.'

'Right,' agreed Simpson. 'I'll get him to send a couple of men to help keep watch on the Sheridan spread in case Durango shows up.'

'Good,' said Webster. 'I'll watch the ranch until they arrive.'

The two men spurred their horses and, as the hoofbeats faded, Mart Webster swung from the saddle and moved to the edge of the hill to keep watch.

When Simpson and Readman reached the Twisted F they knocked on the ranch-house door and were soon admitted to Amos North.

'Well,' he smiled as they entered the room, 'I expected someone before now to tell me Durango was hanging by the neck.' His voice trailed away and his smile vanished when he saw the serious expression on the men's faces. A cold look of anger and annoyance darkened his face. 'What went wrong this time?' he snapped.

In spite of his bulk and outward appearance of tough ruthlessness Curt Simpson was reduced to a trembling heap of flesh when faced by Amos North in the mood which came upon him as he listened to Simpson's story. His eyes blazed with fury and he heaped curses upon all those concerned in the attempted elimination of Durango.

'You'll all pay dearly for this if Durango isn't found and dealt with,' he hissed. 'If it wasn't for me you'd all get nowhere. Remember, Simpson, I tipped you off to extend the Gay Lady – you'll make a fortune when the town grows. Readman, you'll be foreman of the biggest land-owning concern in Texas and the appropriate rewards go with the position. I brought Webster in on deals; he'll be sheriff in a boom town and can make a lot of money on the side. I put you all in these positions but I expect no mistakes in return.' The two men shifted positions uneasily. 'I know that in this case it's largely Mart Webster to blame for Durango's escape but I'll hold you all responsible, if he isn't dealt with.' His eyes narrowed. 'I stand to make a fortune and I'm not going to lose it because of Durango. You told me how nosey he'd been then he comes prowling round here; he must have some suspicions about me...' North paused. He looked thoughtful. 'He could know very little about me from the people around here; in fact I reckon all he could find out would be that I own land to the East and in New Mexico. If you were in a possession of those facts, Simpson and wanted to know more about me what would you do?'

The big man looked thoughtful for a moment. 'I figure I'd either pay New Mexico or Baylor County a visit,' he muttered.

'Right,' agreed North his manner easing somewhat. His mind was cold and calculating as he tried to figure out the best way to deal with Durango. 'And then I reckon I'd choose the easiest ride – that to the east.' His mind raced and the words rapped out as he issued orders. 'Simpson you get back to town and keep an eye on things there, just in case Durango doubles back to Newlin. Readman take two of the boys and return to the Three Rs leave them to keep watch on the ranch and you and Webster try to pick up Durango's trail. Tell Webster what I figure and try to the east.'

The two men nodded and turned to leave. North stopped them.

'Remember, no slip-ups this time,' he warned.

Curt Simpson left the Twisted F at a fast pace and headed for Newlin whilst Floyd Readman hurried to the bunkhouse where he selected two of the toughest cowboys and ordered them to saddle up.

Mart Webster watched the Three Rs ranch-house from the edge of the hill but nothing stirred in the darkness. He saw the light go out in the bunkhouse and a few minutes later that in the ranch-house was also extinguished. He guessed everyone had settled down for the night and yet he wondered. In spite of finding nothing he felt that all was not as it should be. Mart cursed himself for letting Kathy Sheridan put him off searching her bedroom; the only room he had not been in and now when he thought about it, he figured that Mrs Sheridan would not hesitate to hide someone there. Webster decided to investigate.

He slipped down the hillside and crept stealthily towards the buildings. He moved around quietly but after a quarter of an hour realized it was useless. There was not a sign of anyone and as far as the ranch-house was concerned curtains were drawn over most windows and those rooms where the windows were not covered were so dark he could not distinguish anything inside. Of one thing he was certain, no one moved in any of the buildings. Disappointed, Mart Webster returned to keep his vigil from the hillside unaware that Kathy Sheridan knew of his prowling and had warned Vernon Petch to hide.

Some time passed before Mart heard the sound of approaching horses. He eased his Colt from its holster and flattened himself behind some boulders. When he heard the animals slow to a walking pace he peered cautiously from behind his cover and made out the shadowy form of three riders. He hesitated wanting to make sure who it was before he revealed himself.

The riders halted and a moment later a voice called softly, 'Mart.'

Webster recognized Readman's voice. 'Over here,' he answered quietly and then stood up to show himself. The three men turned their horses and walked them to the sheriff.

'Anything happen?' asked Readman as they swung from the saddles.

'No,' answered Mart. 'I took another look around down there but saw no one. How did North take the news?'

'I don't want to face him in that mood again,' replied Readman. 'If he hadn't needed us I reckon he'd hev killed us on the spot. Says we must git Durango or else...' Readman left the words unspoken but their meaning was not lost upon Webster. Floyd went on to relate North's ideas and when he had finished the sheriff had to agree that it was quite possible that Durango had headed east.

'I reckon we'll ride a short way now, camp, then search for his trail in the morning,' said

Webster. He turned to the two Twisted F cowboys. 'Watch the ranch, carefully,' he ordered. 'If Durango shows up don't hesitate to put a bullet in him but I want Petch alive.'

The two men nodded and prepared to settle down whilst Webster and Readman swung into the saddles. They rode along the hillside for about three miles before moving down into the valley to camp for the remainder of the night.

They were up early the next morning and after a quick breakfast rode slowly along the valley weaving back and forth looking for some sign of Durango's passage. They had been searching for about an hour when a shout from Readman brought the sheriff galloping to his side. The foreman of the Twisted F was on his knees examining the ground and Mart Webster dropped from the saddle almost before his horse had stopped.

'Look at this,' said Readman pointing to some hoof marks. 'Two horses passed this way, one appears to be behind the other and I'd say those tracks weren't very old.'

'Good work,' said Webster excitedly. 'They've just got to be Durango and Petch.'

The two men remounted their horses and moved steadily eastward following the trail.

It was mid-morning when it became obvious that the animals which they were following had stopped. There were signs of a small fire, but the two men were puzzled by the fact that there were only one set of footmarks.

'What do you make of it?' asked Readman. Webster pushed back his sombrero and stared at the marks on the ground. He frowned and scratched his head a puzzled look on his face. 'I can't understand it,' he muttered. 'There's one set of horse tracks heading north but the other keeps going east.' Suddenly he looked sharply at Readman, the bewildered look gradually disappearing as if he might have found a solution to his troubled thoughts. 'Supposin' Durango and Petch were at the Three Rs last night and supposin' Amos North is right, that Durango is goin' to make inquiries about him in Baylor County then he wouldn't need Petch with him. Petch has to hide so he leaves him at the Three Rs.'

'But we searched everywhere,' put in Readman.

'Mrs Sheridan put me off searchin' her bedroom,' said Webster, 'I'll bet Petch was there.'

'Then let's go back–' started Readman.

'It's Durango we want,' interrupted Webster. 'Your two men are capable of looking after Petch.'

'Why two horses?' asked Floyd still puzzling over the tracks.

'In case we got on to them at the Three Rs, the double tracks would lead us to believe they both left, beside they couldn't leave a freshly ridden horse around the ranch, it would make it obvious that someone was there.' Webster was excited now; he felt sure he was near the truth. 'I reckon Durango released the other horse here an' I figure we can forget the trail. C'm on Floyd we'll give Johnny Durango a lively time in Baylor County.'

# ELEVEN

Johnny Durango rode slowly up the main street of Seymour the county town of Baylor County. He was glad to have reached the end of his ride and he looked forward to at least one night in a comfortable bed. It was late afternoon and, although he felt sure he was close to the truth about Amos North, he reckoned it would be unwise to start the return journey to Newlin that evening. Both he and his horse would benefit from a rest.

He sought out the livery stable and it was only after making sure that his horse was comfortable and had all it wanted that he thought of himself. Johnny strolled along the sidewalk to the hotel where he booked a room for the night. After freshening up Johnny went to the cafe and enjoyed a meal. Whilst he was anxious to find out about North he wanted to play things safe; if he rushed things too much he might come unstuck. Leaving the cafe he crossed the dusty street to the saloon. There were a number of cowboys standing beside the long mahogany counter and several of the tables were also occupied. As he strolled to the bar Johnny glanced round the big room and reckoned that by the time it was dark it would be crowded.

Durango leaned on the counter and ordered a bottle of whisky and two glasses. A moment later they were in his possession and, picking them up, he strolled to a table at which he had noted an oldish man was sitting.

'Mind if I sit here?' asked Johnny.

The old man looked up. ''Course not son,' he said. There was a smile of welcome in his eyes.

Johnny sat down and pushed a glass towards the man. 'Have a drink with me,' he said and passed the bottle.

The man took the bottle and poured himself a drink. 'That's mighty kind of you,' he said. He scratched his beard thoughtfully, looking at Johnny. 'Stranger around here, aren't you?'

Johnny nodded. 'First time in Seymour,' he replied.

The old man's brown, gnarled face broke into a smile. There was a twinkle in his brown eyes when he spoke. 'Wal, son what is it you want to know?'

Johnny was taken back at the directness of the question. He stared at the man opposite to him, and then his face relaxed into a broad grin. 'You're a shrewd one,' he said. 'I could say I'm just bein' sociable.'

The old man laughed. 'The days of a stranger bein' sociable are passed,' he drawled. 'He's only like that if he wants to know somethin'.'

Durango liked the look of the old man and decided that his best course was to be open with him. He smiled.

'Wal,' he said. 'I was hoping you might be able to tell me something about Amos North.'

The old man looked sharply at Johnny. 'You in trouble with him?' he asked.

'In a way, yes,' replied Johnny. 'I've been making inquires into a murder of a friend of mine and everything leads me to think North was behind it but I can't prove anything. I thought something in North's past might help me. Just tell me what you know.'

'He's the biggest rancher around here, owns a sizeable piece of Baylor County,' he said. 'Owns a good deal of this town. Everything he touches seems to turn to money. Guess you'd say he is a good businessman. Mind you he knows the cattle business inside out. It used to be his father's spread but Amos really built it up into the size it is today.' He paused thoughtfully and poured himself another glass of whisky. 'He'll drive a hard bargain but he's well liked around here, a good boss his cowhands say, a good landlord his tenants will say.'

Johnny detected that the old man was keeping to other people's opinions. 'But what do you think?' he asked.

'Wal, I've had no direct dealings with him,' drawled the bearded man, 'but there's always been something about Amos North that I just didn't like. I've always felt he'd stop at nothing to get what he wanted, mind you I've no reason for sayin' that; his money always talked around here an' he's never been pushed.'

'Did he get everything legally?' asked Johnny.

'Sure, you couldn't trip him up on that score,' came the reply.

'There's been no special reason for buyin' all this land an' property?' asked Johnny.

The old man shook his head. 'Only to extend his ranch and hev a big income from rents,' he answered.'

Johnny looked thoughtful. 'There doesn't seem much to help me in North's life story,' he said. 'Does he spend much time here?'

'Not as much as he used to,' replied the old man. 'I believe he has other property in New Mexico.'

Johnny thanked him and pushed the remainder of the whisky towards him. He started to rise from his chair when the old man put out his hand and stopped him.

'There is one other thing I've just thought of,' he said. 'A few years ago North bought quite a lot of land around Quanah close to the Oklahoma border, bought it cheap sold it at a big profit. It was all very much of a secret and I've never heard it talked about round here but I was in Quanah at the time and I'm certain it was North who put through the deal.'

'Who did he make this deal with?' he asked.

'I'm afraid I don't know,' replied the old man. 'I wasn't much interested in it. North's affairs were his own and as it wasn't known around here I didn't think any more about it. That's all I can tell you son.'

Johnny thanked the man once again and left the saloon. He was very thoughtful as he walked back to the hotel and sought the comfort of his bed. As far as he could see he had gained very little from his visit to

Seymour. There appeared to be nothing in Amos North's past life to give a reason for his purchase of land around Newlin. Johnny could not see the rancher resorting to killing if it was just another case of building up a big ranch. There must be more in it than that if North was willing to have Nick Sheridan and Dan Neale killed and was anxious to get him out of the way.

Johnny's thoughts turned to the information about Quanah. North had put through a deal there and had kept it as much of a secret as possible. This was a similar pattern to what had been going on in Newlin. Maybe the answer lay there; maybe the reason for buying land around Newlin was the same reason for buying it near Quanah. Johnny felt sure it would be worth investigating. His visit to Seymour was probably not a waste of time after all.

Durango left Seymour the following morning and kept to a steady pace as he rode north-westwards towards Quanah. About an hour after he had left town Mart Webster and Floyd Readman, dust-covered and weary, rode into Seymour.

'I figure the first place to check is the hotel,' said Webster. 'If he stayed in town for the night he may have been there.'

The two men swung from their saddles and entered the wooden building. When he heard the door open the clerk put down the paper and climbed from his chair to greet the new arrivals.'

'Rooms gentlemen?' he asked cheerily.

'That depends,' said Webster. 'We're really looking for a friend of ours; we believe he rode into Seymour yesterday so we wondered if he is staying here. His name is Durango.'

'Sure, he was here,' replied the clerk.

'Was?' asked Readman a puzzled frown on his face. 'Has he left then?'

'Left this morning, about an hour ago,' answered the clerk. 'Nice young fella told me he was heading for Newlin but had some business to attend to in Quanah on the way.'

'Quanah?' Webster queried.

'Yeah, that's what he said,' replied the clerk.

'Thanks,' said Webster. 'I reckon we'll catch him up there.'

The two men left the hotel, remounted their horses and rode out of Seymour by the north trail before heading north west for Quanah.

Johnny Durango rode slowly along the main street in Quanah looking for the saloon. It had been a hot ride under the blazing sun and he wanted to slake his throat before starting his inquiries about North. He pulled to a halt outside the false fronted building, swung from the saddle and was tying his horse to the rail when a voice rapped out.

'Hold it, Durango!'

Johnny froze. His thoughts raced; he did not recognize the voice immediately but it had a familiar ring about it. Who knew him in this town? He turned round slowly to find a young man of about his own age grinning at him. Johnny gasped and his face split into a broad smile of surprised pleasure.

'Jed Lucas!' he gasped and jumped forward to greet his old friend. 'Why you old son of a...' he cried grasping Jed's hand and slapping him on the shoulder. 'You're a sight for sore eyes. But what's this?' he added pointing at the tin star pinned to the brown shirt.

'Meet the Sheriff of Quanah,' smiled Jed proudly. 'But what are you doin' here? Last time I saw you was way out in Arizona.'

'You're just the man I want,' he said seriously. 'Let me have a beer and then can we go to your office and talk?'

'Sure, Johnny,' replied the tall, rugged sheriff. You're not in trouble are you?'

'Wal I'm not on the wrong side of the law

if that's what you mean,' answered Johnny. 'Although I've just broken out of jail.'

Jed Lucas pulled up short as he was about to push open the batwings. He stared incredulously at his friend. Johnny looked at him and burst out laughing. The sheriff relaxed, a smile on his face.

'I might have guessed you were pulling my leg,' he said.

'I'm not,' grinned Johnny. 'It's perfectly true. But come on, let's have this drink and I'll tell you all about it.'

Once they had downed their beers the two friends hurried to the sheriff's office. When they sat down Jed handed Johnny a cheroot and once they were lit the sheriff looked questioningly at Johnny and waited for him to begin his story.

Johnny related the facts quickly without leaving out any of the details. 'So you see,' he concluded, 'Amos North seems to be at the back of everything but I have no proof nor can I find any reason for his actions.'

'I think I can give you a reason,' replied Jed quietly.

For a moment, the words did not seem to register in Johnny's mind then suddenly his eyes blazed with excitement. 'You can!' he said; there was a tone of eager anticipation in his voice.

'The old man in Seymour suspected that North was behind some land deals around here,' said Jed. 'Wal, he was right. It was just before my time as sheriff; North did just the same as he is doing in Newlin. He got local people into his scheme, the lawyer, the sheriff and so on in order that he could get tipped off about local conditions and local people. He purchased land legally but various people who wouldn't sell ran into trouble until they were pleased to accept the offer made by North. Mind you he kept in the background and it was only after the whole thing was finished that his name was linked with it, but nothing could be proved against him and that was that.'

'But what did he want the land for?' asked Johnny.

'I'm coming to that,' said Jed. 'And it will give you your reason for what's been happening around Newlin. North sold that land at a fat profit to the railway company!'

'Railway!' Johnny gasped.

'Somehow he got to know which route the company was going to take and bought the appropriate land,' said Jed. 'Another thing I can tell you; the company's aiming to push westwards!'

'It's the same all over again,' cried Johnny excitedly. 'Now, I've got the reason! That valley where Nick Sheridan settled is a natural route for a railway. It will be worth a fortune. No wonder North wants it. Newlin will become a boom town and that's why Curt Simpson enlarged the Gay Lady; he's all prepared to fleece the construction gangs and no doubt North has an interest in that too.' He pushed himself to his feet. 'Thanks Jed, I'm sure glad I ran across you. The sooner I get back to Newlin the better.'

'Glad to have been of help, Johnny,' said Jed. 'But be careful, North will be ruthless if he wants something.'

'I'll watch out,' replied Johnny and took Jed's extended hand in a firm grip.

At the moment two men were riding slowly along the main street of Quanah, their eyes searching everywhere, missing nothing. They pulled to a halt outside the saloon, swung from their horses and after tying them to the rail paused to look along the street.

The door of the sheriff's office swung open and Johnny hurried out, stepped off the sidewalk and set off across the dusty street for his horse still hitched to the rails outside the saloon. Suddenly he froze in his tracks when he saw the two men.

Mart Webster! Floyd Readman! The words flashed through his mind. He could hardly believe his eyes.

At almost the same time Webster and Readman saw Johnny. They stiffened; a tenseness gripped them, now they had found the man they sought to kill.

'Spread out,' whispered Mart and started to move slowly sideways, away from Readman who edged nearer the rail and started to walk slowly along the street.

Johnny's eyes narrowed. He watched the two men carefully. How they had got on to him he did not know, nor did it matter; they were here for one purpose – to kill him so that Amos North would be free to put through his schemes. Johnny tensed himself, his right hand hovered close to the butt of his Colt strapped tightly against his thigh. He eased himself on his feet into a perfect balance and crouched ready for instant action. He was caught in the open; he could not hope to reach any cover. The gap between the two men was widening. Suddenly Mart Webster stopped. This was the moment. A sudden coolness had descended on Johnny and his brain was working calmly and methodically. He could see Mart Webster that first day he saw him in Newlin. Johnny had figured then that the sheriff was good with a gun and now he stood in the centre of the main street of Quanah his talon-like fingers hanging in that deceptive casualness which had fooled many men. Johnny had to admire Mart Webster; he had not sought any cover from which to take Johnny; he relied entirely on his own ability and in that he had great faith.

A quietness had descended on the main street and without looking Johnny knew that, although the situation had been alive for only a few seconds, the atmosphere of an impending gunfight had cleared the street.

Johnny watched Mart Webster closely and at the same time could still keep Floyd Readman in view. Was Webster setting him up for Readman to kill or was he going to take him alone with Readman positioned as a precaution in case Webster slipped up? Johnny's thoughts raced, then he pulled himself up sharply; these two were playing it slow to try to get him on edge and a gun-man on edge was a certain loser. Johnny's thoughts went cold and he concentrated on the two men.

'Durango,' called Webster, 'this is the end for you; I told you it would come to this. You should have taken my warning and moved on that first day.'

'You've ridden a long way to get me,' answered Johnny, 'I guess it must be for something more important than Dan Neale, something like a railroad.'

He saw a reaction on Webster's face but the Sheriff of Newlin did not answer. Readman who had kept moving slowly was almost level with Johnny and any second would not be easy to watch. Johnny saw Webster glance in Readman's direction and then in a flash that casual hang of the hand was gone; so fast that it almost caught Johnny unawares despite his deep concentration on Webster's fingers.

Mart's gun was already clear of its leather when Johnny dived forward slipping his Colt from its holster as he did so. The bullet grazed the top of Johnny's shoulder. As he hit the dust Johnny squeezed the trigger and with Webster standing above him the bullet thudded upwards into Webster's chest. He staggered backwards as if hit by a powerful hand and his second shot screamed harmlessly past Durango. Webster's knees buckled and he pitched into a silent heap in the road. Johnny was already rolling over to bring his gun to bear on Readman but as he did so he saw the foreman of the Twisted F crash backwards against the rail and slide to the ground his Colt slipping from his fingers. Johnny's brain reeled; who had saved him from almost certain death? He pulled himself slowly to his feet and saw the door of the sheriff's office flung open and Jed Lucas strode out with a Colt in his hand.

'Thanks,' said Johnny when the lawman reached him.

'You all right?' asked Jed anxiously.

'Yes,' replied Johnny, 'it's just a nick on top of the shoulder.'

'Saw the set up from the window,' explained Jed. 'Thought these must be two of the hombres you told me about. Had that one covered all the time. Guess you must be on to something pretty big fer them to trail you this far to get you.'

People had drifted back on to the street and the sheriff ordered four men to remove the bodies. Johnny picked up his sombrero and glanced at Webster.

'He sure was quick on the draw,' he murmured. 'He'd hev been a good lawman if it hadn't been for North.'

Half an hour later, his wound having been attended to by the doctor, Johnny Durango left Quanah at a steady pace for Newlin.

# TWELVE

It was early the following morning when Johnny Durango approached the Three Rs ranch and the sound of his horse brought the three hands hurrying from the stables with guns drawn.

They relaxed and reholstered their weapons when they saw Johnny.

'Glad to see you back,' they called as they ran to meet him.

Johnny swung from the saddle. 'Everything all right here?' he asked.

'Couple of visits from Luke Ashton,' replied Wes. 'Got rather nasty the second time, when Mrs Sheridan still refused to sell. Lost control of himself and threatened that the place would be burned over our heads.'

Johnny nodded thoughtfully. 'Saddle me a fresh horse,' he said, 'also one each for Mrs Sheridan and for yourselves. Amos North is in fer a big surprise.' He turned and hurried towards the ranch-house.

He had almost reached the veranda when a rifle crashed from the hillside. Johnny spun round and fell to the ground grasping his arm. He staggered to his feet and dived towards the veranda as the rifle roared again spurting dust. The door of the house was flung open to reveal a wide-eyed, startled Kathy with Vernon Petch by her side. They grasped Johnny as he stumbled forward to the doorway. The three cowboys had raced from the stables and flattened themselves on the ground blazing away at the hillside even though the range was too great to be effect- ive. They gradually eased their firing and when no more shots were forthcoming from the unseen sniper they stopped and scrambled to their feet.

'See to the horses,' ordered Wes, 'I'll find out if Johnny is all right.'

Kathy Sheridan slammed the door once Johnny was inside.

'Johnny!' she gasped. 'Are you all right? I should have known they'd leave someone to watch the ranch.'

Petch examined the wound. 'It will be all right once we've got it bandaged,' he said.

The door opened and Wes Conrad stepped in an anxious look on his face.

'I'm all right, Wes,' smiled Johnny. 'Get the horses ready quickly. It's my guess that who- ever took that shot is already on his way to tell North.'

As Kathy attended to his wound Johnny told both her and Petch about the results of his journey to Seymour and Quanah.

'So that was North's game,' whispered Petch when Johnny had finished his story. 'No wonder he wanted this valley. Mrs Sheridan your land will be worth a fortune. I thought Luke Ashton was anxious to make you sell. He must be on a good thing.'

Kathy Sheridan looked gratefully at Johnny. 'I cannot thank you enough for all you've done,' she said, 'I know that Nick...'

'It's not over yet Kathy,' interrupted Johnny embarrassed by her gratitude. 'Vernon, I want you to ride into Newlin as quickly as possible, tell the deputy sheriff the whole story and tell him to arrest Curt Simpson and Luke Ashton if they are in town. Kathy I'm takin' you over to Stella Neale, I think you'd be safer there than left here on your own; tell her everything and that I feel sure Readman would be the one who killed Dan on North's instructions.'

'What are you going to do Johnny?' Kathy asked anxiously.

'I'm goin' for Amos North,' he answered. 'Wes Clint and Bud'll ride with me because I'm certain North will be waiting for us.'

The sound of the horses coming round from the stables took them hurrying outside and whilst Vernon Petch put his horse up the hillside in the direction of Newlin, Kathy, Johnny and the three cowboys galloped towards the Twisted F.

When they saw Johnny reach the safety of the Three Rs ranch-house the two men from the Twisted F moved away from the edge of the hill and hurried to their horses.

'Think we got him?' queried one of the men.

'Probably winged him enough to keep him quiet for a while,' replied the other. 'North isn't goin' to like it. He wanted him dead but we'll have to let him know.'

They put their horses into a gallop, keeping below the hill-top until it was safe enough to swing in the direction of the Twisted F. They did not spare their mounts in their effort to reach the ranch as quickly as possible. When they reached the house the men leaped from their sweating horses and knocked loudly on the front door. A few minutes later they were being shown into North's study.

Amos North was talking to Curt Simpson who had arrived only half an hour before.

They both turned to the door when the two cowboys hurried in.

'Durango's back,' panted one of the men.

Simpson looked startled but North asked calmly. 'Well, did you deal with him?'

'Winged him, Mister North,' came the reply.

North's face slowly darkened, his eyes narrowed seeming to pierce the two men making them feel his annoyance and contempt.

'Fool, I said kill him,' he hissed. 'I expect my men to be good shots and to obey me implicitly. I'm tired of saying Durango must be got rid of; he seems to bear a charmed life. How badly hit was he?'

'I'm not sure,' muttered one of the men uneasily. 'He got into the house before we could be certain, but I figure he may be laid up.'

'Maybe, maybe,' roared North. 'I don't want any half certainties. I want results and I'm not getting them. This whole business was just about tied up until Durango came on the scene. Now it looks as if I will have to resort to desperate measures to finish it off.' He paused in his pacing up and down. 'Where's Webster and Readman?' he snapped.

'Haven't seen them since they left us to

watch the Three Rs an' went trailin' Durango,' replied one of the cowboys.

North glanced sharply at Simpson who looked uneasy.

'If they hadn't found Durango's trail they'd have been back,' said Simpson. 'If they had found it and he'd given them the slip they'd have still been back. Seems to me Durango's outsmarted them same way as he dealt with Blackie Farrow.'

'What? Two men couldn't take care of him?' There was a note of disbelief in North's voice.

'You don't know this Durango,' replied Simpson testily. 'I saw him operate in the Gay Lady. Some of the slickest shootin' I've ever seen; look what happened in the Palo Duro Canyon, he should hev been out-numbered there.' In spite of his huge bulk and usual tough appearance Simpson was obviously nervous. 'I'm tellin' you,' he went on, 'if Webster and Readman tackled him in the open I'm betting Durango out shot them.'

'Pull yourself together Simpson,' snapped North. 'This man is not super-human; he can be dealt with and I'm certainly not going to let him spoil our plans just when they're about complete. Ashton told me he almost had Mrs Neale selling yesterday. We'll take a ride over there and finally convince her. Then we'll go to the Three Rs, give them the same treatment and settle with Durango.' He turned to the two cowboys. 'Get fresh horses,' he ordered, 'and tell the other six men to saddle up.'

When they had left to carry out his orders North crossed the room and opened a drawer in his desk. He pulled out a well-worn gun-belt. Removing the Colt from its holster he caressed it lovingly. There was an uncanny gleam in his eye as he looked at Simpson.

'That gun brought me a lot of power in the early days,' he said. His voice was low and cold. 'I haven't worn it in anger for a long time but I've kept in practice; I can still draw fast and shoot straight. It seems I picked a lot of fools to carry through my schemes around Newlin. Now I'm going to have to strap this back on and finish things off myself!'

Simpson saw a different Amos North to the man he already knew. Here was a man cold and ruthless, a man who had enlarged his power with a gun and afterwards used the abilities of other men to implement his schemes. Simpson seemed to see him as a criminal for the first time, a man whose fine intelligence had been used by a twisted mind to gain power and money, to satisfy an incessant craving. Now, as he strapped the Colt round his waist and tied the holster tight to his right thigh, he became cold and deadly with death at his finger tips.

'You coming, Simpson?' The words broke into the saloon-owner's thoughts.

'Sure, sure,' he replied. He knew it was useless to do anything else. If North won and he hadn't ridden with him he would be finished; North would see he was destroyed. If Durango won he would be finished anyway so he figured he might as well ride with North and try to make sure North came out on top. It was his only chance of survival. Simpson felt somewhat easier as they galloped in the direction of Neale's spread, ten of them; North could not lose. Even these odds were too much for Durango.

The thunder of their hooves brought Stella Neale and her two hired hands hurrying from the house where they had been discussing the offer made by Luke Ashton the previous day.

'Wonder what this bunch want?' said one of the men.

'I don't know,' said Mrs Neale a little

wearily. 'If it's another offer for the ranch I think I'll take it. I'm tired of everything.'

The two men looked anxiously at her. 'Dan wouldn't have wanted that,' said one of them. 'Remember you said that you didn't believe Johnny Durango killed Dan; folks in town reckon he said he was framed by the Twisted F and some of these cowpokes are from that spread.'

There was no chance of further conversation as the ten riders pulled their horses to a halt in a swirl of dust. As they milled around, the man who led them swung from his saddle and stepped towards Mrs Neale.

'Good day ma'm,' he said touching his hat. 'You won't know me. Mrs Neale,' he said smiling charmingly. 'I'm Amos North from the Twisted F. I don't move off my own ranch much when I am there, but I would like a word with you about Luke Ashton's visit. May I go inside.'

Stella Neale hesitated. This man had been politeness itself but there was something about him which sent a chill through her. Her thoughts raced. What did he know about Luke Ashton and the offers made for the ranch? Why was Curt Simpson riding with him, Simpson, whom Dan and Johnny Durango had suspected was somewhere behind this land buying? And why bring so many riders?

North sensed the hesitation. 'It will only take a few moments,' he hastened to add, 'then we'll be on our way.'

She had no reason to doubt or suspect this man so Mrs Neale's good manners prevailed. 'Come inside, Mr North,' she said and, turning led the way into the house.

'Mrs Neale,' said North once they were inside. 'I'm going to tell you something which only a few people know. When Luke Ashton made those offers for the Circle A and Three Rs he was doing so on my behalf. I understand you refused to sell so I thought I would come into the open and meet both you and Mrs Sheridan personally; I'm riding over there when I leave here; and make you see that under the circumstances it would be far better for you both to sell your property.'

'Why are you anxious to have it?' asked Stella.

'It is imperative that I enlarge my ranch,' lied North, 'and the valley and its approaches are what I want. I'd like you to reconsider.'

Stella smiled, remembering the words of one of her men. So if Durango had been framed by the Twisted F then Amos North must have been behind it and in that case must have been the instigator of the death of her husband. She decided to play for time.

'I'm sorry, Mister North,' said Stella, 'I'm afraid that I must give you the same answer as I gave Mister Ashton, that I'm not prepared to decide just yet. It's too soon after my husband's death and there are many things to sort out.'

North's eyes went cold, a look of annoyance crossed his face but he quickly controlled it. 'Mrs Neale,' he said, 'if you don't decide now I may not be in a position to offer you the same amount later on and may I say that it is a pretty substantial offer I am making.'

'No, I won't sell yet,' replied Stella.

'But Mrs Neale—' began North.

'I have nothing more to say,' interrupted Stella. 'I'd be obliged if you left, I have a lot to do.'

North stiffened. His eyes narrowed. 'You'll regret this,' he hissed. 'I'm going to have the Circle A and have it now!' He spun on his heels, strode to the door and flung it open. His face was black with anger as he stepped outside. 'All right boys you know what to do,' he yelled.

The men immediately turned their horses and split into three groups as briefed by

North on their way to the Circle A. Two galloped to the stables two more went to the bunkhouse and the third pair jumped from their horses and ran to the house. Curt Simpson held his horse steady, dragging his Colt from its holster to cover the two Circle A men but already they were jerking at their guns. Simpson's Colt roared and one man staggered backwards and fell to the ground with a bullet in his stomach. The second man's gun cleared its leather but before he could squeeze the trigger North's Colt had sent lead screaming into the man's back and he crashed to the ground in a huddled heap.

Mrs Neale who had run to the doorway stared aghast at the slaughter which had happened so quickly. Terror was in her eyes when the two cowboys grasped her and pulled her roughly out of the way. As they ran inside the house she flung herself at North.

'Stop it! Stop it!' she screamed.

He pushed her contemptuously to one side. She stumbled and fell to the boards, tears streaming down her eyes, her body shaken by sobs.

North looked down at her angrily. 'You had your chance Mrs Neale,' he snarled. 'Nick Sheridan and your husband were too stubborn about selling so they had to be eliminated.' Stella looked up at him her eyes wild with fear as she realized the man before her was admitting the guilt of two murders. 'Nobody is going to stand in my way of a fortune!'

There was a mad look in his eyes as he turned away and saw smoke pouring from the stables. The frightened whinny of the horses as they thundered from the building seemed to jerk Stella Neale back to reality. Suddenly there was a crash from the house and the two men came running out. Beyond them she saw flames flickering up the curtains. She scrambled to her feet and then, with a cry of anguish, ran into the building. One of the men tried to stop her but she squirmed past him.

'Let her go!' shouted North and ran to his horse.

Flames were leaping from the three buildings. Soon nothing would be left but a smouldering ruin to mark what had once been a happy home. There was an evil smile of satisfaction on Amos North's face as he sat on his horse watching the scene and waiting for the rest of his men to mount their horses.

Johnny Durango led the ride from the Three

Rs at a fast pace. He knew he must get to the Twisted F as quickly as possible but first he had to make sure that Kathy Sheridan was safe. As they came to the top of a short rise the five riders hauled hard on the reins, shaken by the sight which met them. Some distance away across the grassland at the bottom of the long gentle slope smoke was rising from the Circle A buildings. Kathy stifled a cry with her hand and looked wildly at Johnny, her eyes wide with shock. They could see men running for their horses and even from that distance they could make out a huge man astride a horse.

'Must be Simpson!' yelled Johnny. 'Rest could be Twisted F. North's acted quicker than I thought.' As he spoke he glanced at the three cowboys. He saw their grim faces, and knew there was no need to ask them to take on the men below even though they were outnumbered. 'Kathy stay here!' he shouted, and kicked his horse forward down the slope.

He flattened himself in the saddle and hearing the thunder of hoofs behind him knew that Wes, Clint and Bud were bent on settling things with North once and for all. The ground flew beneath the flashing hoofs and the blazing buildings drew nearer very quickly.

When North and his men turned in the direction of the Three Rs they were startled to see four horsemen pounding towards them.

'Durango!' yelled Simpson.

'Cover,' shouted North. 'We outnumber them!'

The men leaped from their saddles and sought whatever cover they could and immediately opened fire at the approaching riders. The range was too great to be effective and when Johnny heard the crash of gunfire he pulled hard on the reins, shouting to his men to turn towards two wagons which stood a short distance from the blazing ranch-house. They flung themselves behind the cover as the bullets from the Twisted F whined around them. As Wes and Bud returned the fire Johnny turned to Clint.

'See anything of Mrs Neale?' he shouted.

Clint shook his head. 'Her two men are dead near the front of the house,' he answered indicating the two bodies. 'As we started from the top of the rise I thought I saw someone run into the house.'

Johnny gasped. 'No one could live in there for long. Cover me; I'm goin' in!'

The three men set up a withering fire, and Wes had the satisfaction of seeing one of his bullets crash into a man's shoulder sending him staggering to the ground. Before the man could drop back behind his cover Bud's Colt found its mark and the man pitched to the ground.

Suddenly Johnny jumped to his feet, and bending double, raced towards the cover of the ranch-house. His three men kept the Twisted F cowboys occupied and Johnny had almost reached his objective before bullets flew in his direction. Dust spurted at his feet and, as he dived for the side of the house, a bullet clipped through his sombrero. He hit the ground and rolled over to be protected from the bullets by the side of the building. He jumped to his feet and raced towards the back of the house. Flames leaped from the roof and he knew it would not be long before the roof collapsed. He turned the corner and flung himself against the back-door bursting it open. Smoke poured out and Johnny was forced back momentarily until the first intense smoke had thinned. Shielding his face he raced into the house and ran to the front room. Furniture burned furiously and the dry beams crackled and spluttered as the flames ran their devouring tongues along them. Johnny glanced round anxiously, searching for Stella

Neale. The smoke rose and swirled thickly in front of him then thinned a little and Johnny saw the sprawling form of Mrs Neale in the middle of the room. He jumped forward, grasped the unconscious woman in his powerful arms and, coughing and spluttering, made his way back to the back door.

He staggered outside and a few yards from the house sank slowly to the ground. Relieved of his burden he knelt, panting for breath, drinking great gulps of clean air into his aching lungs. Gun-shots still came from the other side of the building and Johnny realized they were not out of danger yet. He pushed himself to his feet, slipped his Colt from its holster and cautiously made his way towards the far end of the house, hoping to be able to work his way behind the men from the Twisted F.

'He's trying to circle us,' called North to Simpson when he saw Johnny reach the protection of the ranch-house. He glanced round and saw three of his men close-by. 'Get after Durango,' he shouted.

The men looked uneasy with bullets whining around them, but when North yelled angrily again one man leaped to his feet and raced for the space between the ranch-house and the bunkhouse. He had gone only four paces when suddenly he staggered as a bullet ripped into his side. His legs buckled under him and he pitched forward into the dust. Although North yelled and the Twisted F cowboys increased the rapidity of their fire a few minutes passed before the two men were able to use the covering fire and reach the passage-way safely.

They sprinted between the two blazing buildings, the first man a short distance ahead of the other. Without thinking he ran round the corner and pulled up sharply face to face with Durango. Both men were surprised but Johnny recovered that fraction of a second sooner which meant the difference between life and death. Johnny's Colt roared and the man staggered sideways against the building and slid slowly to the ground his gun slipping from his fingers before it could be fired.

Durango stepped past the body to the corner of the building and was about to move forward when he heard the second man approaching. Johnny tensed himself. The man, hearing no shout after the shot, edged cautiously to the corner. Johnny raised his arm in readiness wishing the man would hurry, for the flames were moving rapidly along the wall and were already too close to be pleasant.

A moment later a face and a hand with a gun held ready appeared round the corner and Johnny acted instantaneously. He brought the barrel of the Colt crashing down on the man's head and at the same time grabbed the man's wrist jerking him forward. As the man stumbled past him Johnny struck again with his Colt and the man fell face downwards in the dust.

Durango sprinted across the intervening space between the two buildings and moved quickly along the back of the bunkhouse, which was a mass of roaring flames. Reaching the corner he swung round towards the front which he reached without mishap. He dropped to the ground and inched his way forward until he was able to see round the corner. Both parties were keeping up a steady shooting. A short distance away North and Simpson were using a water-trough for cover. Taking careful aim Johnny squeezed the trigger of his Colt gently. The bullet splintered the wood between the two men whom Johnny wanted alive if possible.

Startled by the unexpectedness of the shot both men twisted round, gasping with amazement when they saw Durango behind them.

'Throw down your guns!' yelled Johnny.

Simpson snarled like some cornered animal and in spite of his bulk moved swiftly to bring his Colt to bear on Johnny. Durango fired and the bullet hit the saloon-owner high in the shoulder. Even as Simpson was squeezing the trigger Johnny was rolling over and the bullet crashed harmlessly into the ground. Johnny's second shot caught Simpson in the chest but even then the huge man seemed to draw extra life from somewhere. He emptied his Colt at Durango who kept rolling over and over until he saw Simpson reel and thud to the ground. Johnny aimed his Colt at North whose attempt to get a shot at Johnny had been impeded by Simpson. Both men fired together and Johnny felt a searing pain as the bullet furrowed the side of his arm but he saw North's gun spin from his hand. The man grasped his shattered fingers and cringed behind the water-trough, his eyes widening with fright. For the first time he found himself at the mercy of another man.

'Call off your men,' yelled Johnny who sent another bullet whining close to North.

'Stop firing!' shouted North. There was a tremor in his voice but he made sure his men heard him.

'Tell them to throw down their guns and step out with their hands up,' called Johnny.

North did as he was told, and when the Three Rs cowboys saw what was happening they broke from their cover and moved towards the Twisted F men, keeping them covered with their Colts.

Johnny pushed himself to his feet and ran to North whom he dragged unceremoniously from the ground.

'You're finished, North!' snapped Johnny, hatred in his eyes. 'I'll see you swing at the end of a rope. Kathy Sheridan and Stella Neale will benefit from the coming of the railroad but even that won't compensate them for the loss of their husbands.'

North did not speak. All the arrogance and swagger had drained from him, leaving in their place dejection and miserable resignation to defeat.

As Bud and Clint shepherded the Twisted F men together Wes ran to Johnny.

'You all right?' he asked anxiously.

'Just a nick in the arm,' answered Johnny and then looked questioningly at Wes. 'Anyone else hurt?' he asked.

'Bud caught it in the shoulder, but it's not serious,' replied Wes.

'Good,' said Johnny. 'Get the horses organized whilst I see how Mrs Neale is, then we'll take this bunch into town.'

Johnny hurried to the back of the smouldering house and found Stella Neale just regaining consciousness.

'Take it easy, Mrs Neale,' said Johnny, dropping on one knee beside her.

Stella smiled wanly at him. 'What happened?' she whispered. Almost immediately a look of horror crossed her face as her mind cleared and the events flooded in upon her. She grasped Johnny's arm tightly. 'Those men...' she gasped. 'Killed...' She turned her head and shuddered when she saw the remains of her home still burning. Her eyes widened, then she sank against Johnny sobbing uncontrollably.

Johnny held her and let her cry, realizing it would do her more good than all the consolation he could offer. Five minutes passed before the sobbing ceased and Stella looked up at him.

'I'm sorry,' she whispered, brushing her hair away from her face.

'That was the best thing you could do,' smiled Johnny reassuringly. 'Don't worry, things will turn out all right. We've caught Amos North and his men.'

He helped Stella to her feet and, with his

arm supporting her, walked to the front of the house where the cowboys from the Three Rs were keeping a close watch on the Twisted F men.

'All right, git mounted!' ordered Wes Conrad when Johnny appeared.

North and his cowboys climbed into the saddle knowing it would be useless to try to escape with Colts trained on them. Wes led two horses to Johnny and helped Stella Neale into the saddle as Kathy Sheridan, who had witnessed the outcome of the fight from the top of the hill, galloped up. There was concern on her face as she halted her horse alongside Stella.

'Are you all right?' she asked.

Stella nodded.

'You'd better ride into Newlin with us,' said Johnny. 'I think it would be as well if you took Stella to see the doctor.'

Kathy agreed, and when the group of riders headed for town Stella glanced at the ruins of her house.

'What am I going to do now?' she whispered half to herself.

Her words were heard by Johnny and he gave the question much thought during the ride to Newlin.

When the riders reached town they

attracted a great deal of attention and by the time they pulled to a halt outside the sheriff's office a large crowd had gathered. Vernon Petch and the deputy sheriff hurried from the office to meet them.

'Glad to see you Johnny,' grinned Vernon. 'I see everything went all right.'

'Sure did,' replied Johnny as he swung from the saddle, 'except that Stella's place got burned down.' Johnny turned to Kathy. 'Take Stella to the doc's; Bud, you'd better go with them. I'll join you in a few minutes.'

Bud nodded and escorted Kathy and Stella to Doc Fleming's house.

'We got Ashton,' said Petch, 'but we found no trace of Simpson.'

'He was with North,' explained Johnny, 'and was killed at the Circle A.'

Once North and his side-kicks were behind bars Johnny relaxed.

'I'm mighty grateful to you, Durango,' said the deputy sheriff. 'I had no idea Mart was on a crooked deal.'

'Of course you hadn't,' reassured Johnny. 'The gang covered up cleverly but they forgot that someone might get curious about Nick Sheridan's death.'

Johnny sent Wes and Clint for a drink, telling them that he would give them a call when he was leaving town. He then hurried to Doc Fleming's where he found that the doctor had examined Stella Neale.

'There's nothing a few days rest won't put right,' said the doctor, 'and Kathy has insisted that Stella goes back to the Three Rs with her.'

'Good,' said Johnny. 'Now, what about Bud?'

'He'll be all right,' reassured the doctor. 'I've only got to finish dressing his wound, then I'll take a look at you.'

'I've been a regular visitor since I rode into Newlin,' grinned Johnny.

Half an hour later Johnny called Wes and Clint from the saloon and the party headed for the Three Rs.

Johnny was preoccupied with his thoughts during the ride, and when they reached the ranch-house he stopped Kathy before she swung from her horse.

'I've got one or two suggestions to make,' he said. 'Mind if Wes, Clint and Bud come in to hear them?'

'Of course not,' replied Kathy. 'Come over, boys, when you've got the horses to the stable, we'll have some coffee ready.'

As Kathy and Stella went into the house the four men led the horses to the stable.

Three-quarters of an hour later, when they were enjoying some coffee, Kathy looked curiously at Johnny.

'Well, Johnny,' she said, 'what are these ideas you have?'

'Maybe you'll tell me its none of my business,' said Johnny, 'but I am rather concerned about what is going to happen to you and Stella. North has finished his career and will hang for it, and the Twisted F is going to be requiring a new owner.' He paused. 'I'd like to suggest that you and Stella throw in together. You'll make a heap of money from the sale of land to the railroad; you'd be able to buy the Twisted F and still have plenty left. With the three ranches joined together you'd have the biggest spread in these parts. You've three good men in Wes, Bud and Clint; make Wes top foreman with Bud and Clint as his right-hand men. I'm sure you'd have no trouble in hiring other cowboys.'

Kathy smiled when Johnny finished. 'Sounds a good idea to me, how about you Stella?'

Stella nodded. 'Nick and Dan would like that,' she said. 'I've nowhere else to go, and it will give us something to work for.'

'Good,' said Kathy. She turned to her

three men. 'What about it?'

They grinned back at her. 'It suits me fine,' replied Wes, 'but I reckon Johnny ought to have my job.'

'Just what I was thinking,' said Kathy, 'but I'm glad you suggested it.'

Everyone looked at Durango. He smiled. 'I'm mighty grateful,' he said, 'but I don't like being tied down. I'm a drifter at heart but I'll be around from time to time. Maybe you wouldn't mind running a few head of cattle for me just as some sort of security when the wanderlust leaves me.'

Kathy crossed the room to Johnny and kissed him lightly on the cheek. 'It is we who are in your debt,' she said sincerely. 'There will always be cattle here belonging to you; come back and claim them often.'

The publishers hope that this book has given you enjoyable reading. Large Print Books are especially designed to be as easy to see and hold as possible. If you wish a complete list of our books please ask at your local library or write directly to:

**Dales Large Print Books**
Magna House, Long Preston,
Skipton, North Yorkshire.
BD23 4ND